CROSSROADS
OF
Darkness

HAZEL WATSON MYSTERY BOOK FOUR

C.A. VARIAN

Contents

Prologue

CAN YOU SEE ME?

"**D**o you want to use my headphones?" Tate asked as he tucked his backpack into the space beneath the seat in front of him.

It would be three hours before they landed in Las Vegas to get married. Candy, Hazel's spirit best friend, and Jake, Candy's spirit lover, blinked out to conserve energy during the flight, but they were in tow and excited about the trip, even if they were ghosts and couldn't be seen by any of the other passengers.

"No, it's okay. I'd rather watch the movie." Leaning over, Hazel placed a kiss on Tate's lips before cuddling up next to him with the pillow and blanket they'd brought from home.

Tate's family understood why they wanted to tie the knot in Vegas and requested they have a small family get together once they returned home to New Orleans. It was a small price to pay so they could save money on a wedding and not have to go through all the planning and all the entertaining that went along with throwing a large party. Hazel wasn't much of a planner, or much of a partier. Just the thought of a large Cajun wedding made her skin itch.

They had an appointment at a small wedding chapel, as well as reservations at a hotel on the strip, and they were excited to spend a few days in a new city, just enjoying each other. They were also excited to do it all without the murder cases that usually plagued their lives, with Tate being a New Orleans police officer and Hazel being able to communicate with the dead. She only hoped no murder victim spirits found her in Vegas and stalked her until she helped them. Candy aside, she really needed a break from ghostly activity.

Finding a movie on the small televisions in front of them, they purchased the airplane headphones and plugged in to watch the movie together.

Turbulence rocked the plane violently, pulling Hazel out of her slumber as the overhead bins began swinging open, losing their contents onto the floor. The pilot asked them to remain calm and fasten their seatbelts, claiming the storm would pass quickly, but she wasn't convinced. Her heart hammered in her ears as she reached for Tate's hand, looking for comfort and reassurance, but her fiancé wasn't there. Her chest became heavier as the sour taste of dread rose into her throat.

Where is he? The bathroom?

Frantically, Hazel tried to look over the seats behind her, but she couldn't see the bathroom doors over the other panicking people who sat between her and the back of the plane. She wouldn't be able to see with her seatbelt holding her in place, but she was ordered to keep it on. Fighting with what to do, she tried to steady her breaths. A baby a few aisles away was screaming and crying, making her anxiety worse. Hazel swallowed thickly, but the taste of dread remained.

She had to take off her seatbelt; she had to find him. Tate could be in danger if he was stuck in the bathroom when the turbulence was too violent. Taking in a deep breath and releasing it slowly, Hazel slipped off her seatbelt and rose from her seat, turning to look behind her. The sound of her heartbeat had become a steady buzzing in her ears. The plane was empty.

Where is everyone? How is the plane empty?

She spun around to look at the seats in the plane's front, but they were empty as well. A chill ran down the center of her body, numbing her. Leaving her seat, Hazel stumbled into the aisle, unsure where she could go but knowing she needed to leave. The seats were empty. Tate was missing.

What was that?

The sound of humming came from the last aisle, but she couldn't see who was making the sound. Holding her breath, she crept toward the voice.

Chestnut hair in pigtails appeared over the back of the second to last seat. She hesitated, too afraid to approach the girl. The humming stopped and was replaced by a low "Can you see me?"

Hazel's breath hitched, and nausea rose in her throat. Approaching the back row of seats, her blood ran cold.

"Bella?"

CHAPTER ONE
Viva Las Vegas

The plane touched down on the runway in Las Vegas and Hazel wriggled awake as she stretched her limbs as best she could, given the limited space in the coach section. Her dream had been unsettling, but that's all it was. It was only a dream. At least she hoped that's all it was as her fiancé, Tate Cormier, leaned across the armrest separating them and placed a kiss on her lips. She closed her eyes, willing the intoxicating taste of him on her lips to replace the memory of seven-year-old Bella, as well as the three spirits she had just found justice for---spirits that included Bella's mother.

"Did you have a good nap, love?" The happiness in Tate's face filled her with giddy delight. She still couldn't believe he was hers after all the years she'd spent wanting him.

Leaning over, she kissed him again as the plane pulled into its parking position. "I did. I didn't realize how tired I was. Did you sleep?"

"A little. Are you excited about tomorrow?"

The seatbelt light had turned off and passengers readied their belongings to exit the plane, but she wasn't in a rush to leave at the moment. Tate held her eyes while the rest of the world moved around them. His blue-gray eyes watched her with delighted amusement.

"I am very excited to be your wife," she said as she handed him the pillow and blanket so he could put them in their backpack.

Huffing a breath and watching for an opening in the people hurrying down the aisle, Tate reached out his hand to her and pulled her to her feet. The rest of their party, Candy and Jake, were waiting for them as they arrived at the terminal. Since Candy and Jake were both spirits, they didn't have to bother with waiting in line or grabbing their belongings. Instead, they could simply vanish from one location and appear in another. Candy approached Hazel as she and Tate walked together, throwing her icy arm around Hazel's shoulders.

"So... where to go first, doll?" Candy asked, as they made their way to the baggage claim.

Hazel wriggled her eyebrows, making Candy whoop into a laugh. "I think we're going to check into the room and get some rest before we do anything else. What are y'all's plans?"

She looked ahead, although Candy and Jake were standing to her left. The last thing she wanted was for airport patrons to see her speaking to empty space. After a few months of living together, Tate had gotten used to Hazel and Candy's conversations, conversations where he could only hear one side.

"Jake and I'll give you lovebirds some space. So, we will either explore the strip or hang out in our room as well. But tonight... Tonight we get to party. Right?"

Hazel hated partying, but it never stopped Candy from asking.

A group of people had already begun crowding the baggage claim area as they arrived. Tate let go of Hazel's hand and wrapped his arm around her waist, placing a kiss on the top of her head.

"Is Candy plotting over there?" he asked, his eyebrow arching.

"Always."

Candy was always plotting. Having been murdered at only twenty-three years old by her boyfriend's stalker, Candy had been taken from her life long before she was ready. Not that anyone could truly be ready to die. She'd been a New Orleans bartender and was living her life to the fullest when the woman snapped, following her home and stabbing her as she entered her apartment.

Hazel had met the spunky crimson-haired spirit when she moved into her downtown New Orleans apartment a few years prior. They'd become fast friends, kindred spirits, some would say. Although Hazel wasn't a party girl and could be seen as more introverted than was healthy, they'd been there for each other in every way that mattered, helping each other grow into better versions of themselves. Candy and Hazel lived in that tiny apartment together, the word *lived* being used loosely since Candy was no longer alive but had recently moved out when Hazel got engaged to her boyfriend and long-time friend, Tate.

Tate couldn't see their ghostly friends, but he had met Candy before she died. It was Tate who'd been called to the scene when Candy was bleeding out in her apartment. He'd tried to save her, all the emergency personnel had, but she'd died in his arms. Tate hadn't figured out the connection until Hazel came clean with him about her abilities, nearly a year after moving into the apartment where she'd met Candy.

Even before Tate had realized she was being haunted by a woman he'd tried to save, Hazel had seen Candy's memory of that night. She'd seen it more often than she'd liked, not that any amount of time was easy to bear. The vision of Candy's spirit cowering in the corner, watching herself bleed to death as he tried to save her, always tore Hazel's heart in two.

Most spirits intentionally sent their memories to her, but Candy didn't. She didn't want Hazel to see any of those things, knowing they would torment her best friend. But their connection was a real, tangible thing, so Candy couldn't stop her mind from sharing her deepest thoughts with Hazel, no matter how badly she wanted to. Hazel knew Tate lived with the same memory, although they tried not to talk about it. It was best, for Candy especially, to not bring up the worst day in her life. Hazel pushed the thoughts away. They were too painful.

She and Tate had known each other since they were freshmen in college, although they'd only recently gotten into a romantic relationship. He was a New Orleans police officer and an all-around good guy, a very sexy good guy. Tate was the one person who never doubted Hazel when she told him about her ability to communicate with spirits and her need to aid those spirits in finding peace so they could leave the world of the living and go into the veil. He also seemed to always forgive her when those same spirits got her into precarious situations that he often had to rescue her from. It happened more often than she'd like to admit.

Having had the ability to communicate with the dead since she was a child, Hazel had always been a loner. The only people she knew who had the same abilities were her mother and her long-dead grandmother. Her father took issue with their second sight. So, it only made sense for her to keep her otherworldly capabilities a secret until she'd fallen in love with Tate. She always believed he would run screaming when he found out, but he hadn't. Instead, he'd loved her, taken care of her, and even proposed to her. So now they walked hand in hand to get married and put everything else behind them. Everything else besides the ghosts. They wouldn't let her push them aside. Ever.

The past few months had been less than ideal. Although their relationship had been amazing, Hazel's life had otherwise been turbulent. She'd been caught up in multiple murder cases and had been in the sights of more than one serial killer. It wasn't something that should be on anyone's resume. Having worked as a public defender, it was expected of her to rub elbows with criminals. But it was not her career that got her involved with killers, it was her gift. Murder victims seemed to be drawn to her and were incredibly persistent. She had learned more than once that serial killers would do anything to get away with murder, and that included silencing her. So, Hazel ended up quitting her job as a public defender, giving herself more time to help the victims who needed her, without the strain of a demanding career on top of it all. Thankfully, with Tate's offer to support her, and the money Candy had saved before her death and given to her only recently, Hazel was able to quit the career she hated.

Arriving at their hotel a short time later, Hazel and Tate said goodbye to their friends and checked into their suite. Another room had been rented for the spirit couple, who always seemed to tag along. They fully intended to do some honeymooning of their own. Hazel just hoped the walls were thick enough to drown out the sounds. Tate placed their luggage on the stand while Hazel unpacked her clothes. They intended to stay in Vegas for a week, taking a few days to rent a car and see some sights. It was their first real vacation together, and they were both excited to enjoy it.

Pulling a shirt and pants from her suitcase—because she was not one to wear girly attire like her best friend—Hazel made her way to the bathroom to get cleaned up. She intended to go into the shower, but before she made it through the threshold, Tate had darted across the room and grabbed her elbow.

"And where are you off to?" Spinning her around, he dipped her as his lips brushed hers. The kiss warmed her from the inside out. He always had that effect on her.

"Going to get cleaned up. Why? Do you want to join me?" Tate's responding grin was purely wicked, wicked enough to elicit a tingle in very sensitive places. She hoped to always be so wanted.

"Maybe," he drawled, lengthening the word. He still held her in place, his arms wrapped tightly around her back. "Race you to the tub!" Tate let go of her so quickly that she thought she would fall, but she recovered, laughing as she followed him to the bathroom. He beat her there, of course, and had already started running water in the large soaking tub by the time she walked through the door.

Hazel couldn't help but lean against the doorframe and soak in the view as Tate removed his shirt. He was scrumptious, and she still couldn't believe he was hers. Her worthiness never seemed to click.

"Are you just going to stand there? Or do you want to climb into this deliciously hot water with me?"

His voice caught her by surprise. Evidently, she'd been so lost in ogling him she had zoned out completely. She blushed and moved forward, discarding her clothes along the way.

"I, one hundred percent, want to climb into that delicious water. Especially with you."

Tate's mischievous smile nearly brought her to her knees as he kicked his pants off and reached out a hand to her, guiding her into the large tub.

CHAPTER TWO

Do Not Disturb

Candy's head popped in through Hazel and Tate's hotel room door before they'd even gotten dressed from their tumble in the sheets. Their kisses and touches in the warmth of the large tub led to more kissing and touching against the bathroom counter, and then even more kissing and touching on the king-sized bed afterwards. Hazel could still feel the tingling in her face from all the times he'd driven her body over the edge. Her friend knew exactly what they could have been doing in their suite, but it never stopped her from barging in.

Candy's eyes were covered, but Hazel would never get used to spirits popping in through walls and locked doors. They didn't have to abide by the same laws of physics as living people did, and many of them liked to exploit that fact. Candy liked to exploit that fact. Hazel pulled the blankets over her and Tate's naked bodies. It was well known that Candy fully intended to catch Tate naked at some point. Even Candy's own boyfriend, Jake, thought her quest was amusing.

"Ever heard of knocking?" Tate covered his face at Hazel's words. He never knew when Candy was around, but he knew of the flirty spirit's intentions all too well. Candy wasn't actually interested in Tate, she just enjoyed making Hazel uncomfortable.

Candy uncovered her eyes and smirked. "I've heard of it, doll, but my hand isn't exactly solid. Not that I would knock, anyway."

"Where's Jake? Does he not want in on this action?" Hazel was beginning to take on more of the "if you can't beat them, join them" philosophy with Candy. It was all in good fun. If Candy wanted to flirt with her man, then surely Hazel could do the same. Although she was admittedly terrible at flirting, even if she'd gotten much better at basic human conversation over the past year.

Reaching her arm back through the wooden door as though it wasn't there, Candy pulled a dark-haired male through the solid surface. Jake, being much shyer than his girlfriend, could not have been blushing much harder when he saw Hazel and Tate in the bed with the blanket to their chins. Even though they were spirits, they appeared as they had in life to Hazel, so the color on his face was obvious. Candy rolled her eyes at him. "He wouldn't stop talking about giving y'all 'privacy,' whatever that means." Candy made air quotations for effect. "He should know by now that there is no such thing when we're together."

Boy, wasn't that the truth?

Even giving Candy her own room in Tate's three-bedroom house hadn't been a deterrent when Candy wanted Hazel's attention. Having a spirit best friend was like having a toddler. A very boy-crazy, overly energetic, nosy toddler who dressed like a bombshell every moment of the day. A toddler who had no shame, no censor, and could pass through any wall or doorway when she wanted to.

Hazel rolled her own eyes, since she and Candy's best friend relationship resembled that of middle schoolers more than a friendship between two grown women. Her temperament improved when she caught Jake's eye and smiled at him, the gesture only slightly snarky. "Thank you, Jake, for at least trying to set boundaries for her. My attempts have never worked."

The flush of Jake's skin only darkened as he lifted his hand to his face and shook his head. Candy was a handful, but he loved her. He loved her so much that he'd remained behind to spend his afterlife with her on the plane of the living, instead of crossing to whatever lay beyond. Hazel wasn't sure if he regretted that decision, but she never asked. "It doesn't work that well for me either," he said, his tone exasperated.

"Did she see anything?" Tate's face was a similar shade to the other man in the room, although one was living, and one wasn't. Candy snickered, but Hazel felt like she was smack dab in the middle of a sitcom and the live studio audience was about to laugh at any moment.

"I don't think so, but she still hasn't said why she barged in." Hazel narrowed her eyes at her best friend, who had now come forward to sit on their bed. Boundaries weren't even in Candy's vocabulary.

"I'm just checking to see if you two are ready to go out. I'm ready to hit the strip."

The blues of Candy's eyes sparkled with wonder, but Hazel sighed with obvious annoyance. She had no interest in going out. She never did. "Assuming you won't take no for an answer?"

Candy glanced side-long at her as though her response was the craziest thing she'd heard all day. "Not in a million years, doll. We're in Vegas! You can stay in bed all day when we're back home!" It was only right that Hazel stuck out her tongue at the feisty spirit.

"How about you and Jake go back to your room so we can get dressed? Then we can go."

Jumping from the bed as though she had a corporeal body, Candy grabbed Jake by the hand and the two spirits darted into the hallway.

"I guess there's no chance of staying in," Hazel said as she turned to face Tate. "Maybe we should have left the ghosts at home."

Take chuckled and wrapped his muscled arm around her, pulling her in close and nuzzling into her neck. He never seemed to be able to resist touching her, and she loved it. "That would have been impossible. You know she would've stowed away, invited or not."

Tossing off the blankets with a groan, Hazel planted her feet on the ground. "You're right, so now we have to entertain her."

Going out with Candy had been a bad idea. The last thing Hazel wanted was to be hungover at her own wedding, but as she stumbled toward her and Tate's hotel suite while hanging onto her his arm, she knew that was exactly what was going to happen. By the time they'd gotten back into the safety of their room, Hazel couldn't do much but flop onto the bed, Tate's warm body sliding up against her. His arm draping over her waist was the last thing she remembered before falling asleep.

CHAPTER THREE

First Day of Forever

*T*he chime of the fasten seatbelt sign stirred Hazel awake after what only seemed like moments of sleep. It was dark in the plane's cabin. All that lit up the space was the strip of lights down the aisle and the occasional light above a seat. It was cold. Icy, even. She rubbed her hands against her arms to warm them while she looked for Tate, who was no longer in the seat next to her. Stretching her back, Hazel glanced toward the bathrooms in the back of the plane, but the only slightly illuminated darkness threw most of the cabin into shadows.

The realization that she'd had a similar experience before hit Hazel like a freight train. She *knew she wasn't awake, but she also realized it wasn't completely a dream. It was something else.*

Unlatching her seatbelt, she stood slowly, bracing her hands on the back of the seat. She scanned the surrounding space, but she knew she wouldn't find Tate. She was looking for Bella.

The plane jolted, nearly tossing Hazel into the aisle. She braced herself on the back of the seat again, lowering herself until she was almost sitting, until the jerking motion of the turbulence calmed. Fear didn't drive her. She knew she wasn't really on the plane. She wasn't in danger. Instead, her jaw set with determination and she stood again. She had to find Bella.

The seven-year-old child had been visiting her dreams increasingly over the past few months, ever since Bella's mother had been murdered and haunted Hazel, infiltrating her life like a disease she couldn't rid herself of. Hazel had ended up solving Emily's murder, along with the other murders committed by the same man, even saving one woman who was his next victim. She'd watched as Bella's mother crossed over to whatever waited beyond the veil. After that, she no longer saw the mother's spirit, but the child had somehow continued to enter Hazel's subconscious mind.

Bella, Emily's child, had gifts, powers Hazel didn't understand. Spirits had infiltrated Hazel's dreams to show her their memories a long time before. It helped her to solve their murders, or to help them with any unfinished business that was keeping them from moving on. She helped them, but it also traumatized her. Watching someone be tortured and killed was never easy on her mind, especially not when it usually played in her mind as though she were the victim.

Even with all the spirits could do, Bella was a living person. A seven-year-old child shouldn't have the ability to enter her dreams and speak to her as though they were there together in some other plane of existence. None of it made any sense to Hazel, but she wanted to understand, needed to understand. It wasn't as though she could contact Bella's father and tell him that his young daughter was stalking her in her dreams. He would probably contact the authorities on her, thinking she was insane. Her only option was to confront the child in their mutual space, in the darkness of her subconscious mind.

The plane shook violently, forcing the overhead bins open and several pieces of luggage to the ground before Hazel chanced standing again.

"Bella?" Hazel's voice echoed in the darkened vacuum around her, the hair on her arms rising with the eeriness of it. The plane shook again, forcing her to bend her knees and brace herself to avoid falling. Even if she wasn't really on a plane, the violent turbulence was scaring the shit out of her. Flying already made her nervous, and the ominous dreams weren't helping.

As the tremor faded, Hazel straightened her legs and stood again, looking toward the back of the plane, toward where she'd seen Bella before. It only took a moment before she saw the little girl.

All was dark, except for the overhead light that shone down on the brown pigtails of Bella, seated in the second to last row on the right. The child looked up slowly, a toothy smile on her face.

"You found me."

"Hazel, wake up." Leaning over her, Tate jostled her shoulders gently, pulling her from her dream and the potential answers the little girl could have given her. She opened her eyes, feeling more annoyed than her face let on, not disappointed to see Tate, but disappointed to be woken from her dream before she could speak to the child.

"Tate." She rubbed her eyes, her head heavy from the late night of drinking. "Is everything okay? What's wrong?"

Leaning against the headboard, Tate wiped the hair off her forehead. "You were flailing in the bed, love." He frowned. "Was it another spirit?"

He couldn't hide the disappointment on his face, and Hazel knew exactly why he was concerned. He had supported her through every haunting, through every spirit-led journey she was sent on that usually got her into some predicament or another. But it was the day of their wedding, and she couldn't let anyone ruin it. Not a spirit, and not a child.

She took his hand, lacing their fingers together, and kissed his knuckles. "It wasn't a spirit. It was just a regular nightmare."

Tate slid back in the bed next to her, pulling her close. "Are you just saying that because you think that's what I want to hear?"

Hazel glared at him, but his crooked eyebrow was too charming to ignore. It made her giggle. "It wasn't a spirit. I promise."

She wasn't lying. Bella wasn't a ghost. Although she realized seeing Bella in her dreams could be just as bad of an omen, she had no way to know until she spoke to the child. She leaned in to kiss him, lingering as she could feel the warmth of his lips spread throughout her body.

"My eyes are covered, but I heard y'all talking." A head of red hair popped into their suite through the wall. "I'm just checking to see what time we're heading out."

Hazel stared at her friend for a moment, still not knowing what time it was herself. Still half asleep, she reached for her cell on the side table. It was nearly noon.

"We don't have to be there for four hours, Candy."

Tate followed Hazel's line of sight to Candy, as he always did, even though he didn't have the ability to see her. And although he couldn't hear her either, it never stopped him from talking to her and trying to include her in things. "How excited are you, Candy?"

The spirit's resounding squeal was the only response they got before the rest of her body slid through the wall and landed on their bed as though the structure had given birth to her. Hazel laughed and scooted out of her way once the icy chill of Candy's form washed over her. She rested her back against Tate's chest, turning and giving him a kiss. "I think she's excited, possibly more than we are."

"I don't think that's possible," he said as he wrapped his arms around her. The scent of his skin almost made her forget the dreamy-eyed intruder on their bed.

"Say, Candy, where's Jake?"

Just as Hazel asked, a head of brown hair, followed by a handsome face with dark-rimmed glasses, slid into their room through the same wall Candy had come through. He didn't plop onto the bed, however, and instead sat in a nearby chair. He and Candy tended to use the furniture as they should, even if neither of them had a physical body.

"Good morning, Hazel," Jake said with a charming smile on his face. "And tell Tate good morning as well."

Candy moved to sit on her lover's lap, kissing him as Hazel passed on Jake's message. How different Candy and Jake were from each other, always surprised Hazel. Candy was outgoing and energetic, and Jake was much more reserved. Regardless, the couple was absolutely in love with each other.

Although they were both now spirits, Candy and Jake had been a couple in life, murdered by the same woman only a few years apart. The woman, Harmony, had stalked Jake for a while, killing Candy out of jealousy before killing Jake for rejecting her. Candy was the first person Jake's spirit had gone to after his murder, and they'd been together ever since. Hazel always worried Jake would move on someday, to wherever spirits were meant to go, forcing Candy to make the decision to leave her or let go of him, but Hazel hoped that would never happen. She would never be ready to let Candy go, as selfish as she knew that was.

CHAPTER FOUR

Warning Before the Chapel

S hortly after they'd arrived, Hazel was able to shuffle their spirit guests back to their room so she and Tate could ease into their wedding day morning. She still had a massive headache and was in desperate need of coffee, as well as a little alone time with her fiancé. So, once Candy and Jake were safely back next door, she and Tate ordered room service and returned to their bed. Before Hazel realized it, sleep had overtaken her again.

"You found me." Bella sat next to her in the back of the darkened plane.

The dream picked up from where it had left off that morning. She realized that fact the minute she looked over to see Bella sitting beside her.

The little girl was so tiny, sitting in the airplane seat. Her legs didn't reach the ground, so they swung playfully. She wore a blue jean dress over a pink t-shirt. Matching pink flip-flops hung from her swinging feet.

"Hazel?" Bella's child-like voice pulled Hazel out of her thoughts. She didn't know how long she'd been sitting there next to the girl, vacantly staring at the child's swinging feet. The little girl looked at her with expectant eyes, waiting for Hazel to acknowledge her.

"I did find you." Hazel swallowed through the tightness in her chest as the plane gave a violent jolt. She knew she wasn't in any danger, but the entire situation still felt wrong. It felt dangerous. "What I don't understand, Bella, is how I found you. I don't understand why you and I are here."

Bella seemed to be expecting Hazel's comment. The child was special, wise beyond her years. Even her mother, Emily, had admitted that to Hazel when she'd spoken with her in spirit form. When Bella had been abducted by her mother's killer, the little girl had used her own otherworldly abilities to get herself rescued.

Months before, it was Bella's father's best friend who had killed her mother and then abducted Bella, causing a standoff on her parents' property between the killer, Hunter, and her father, Joshua. Emily had used her abilities as a spirit, and Hazel's abilities to see through a spirit's eyes to rescue her daughter. Emily forced Hazel to fall unconscious and then connected with Hazel as she went into the house to get details that would help the police disable *the deranged man while simultaneously rescu-ing the child.*

Through Emily's eyes, along with her daugh-ter's powers, they were able to concoct a plan where Bella would go into the bathroom and allow the police to disable her captor while she was pulled through the window. Hunter then got arrested and Bella was saved. It was a high-ly dangerous situation, but because of the com-bined abilities of Emily, Hazel, and Bella, it was resolved with no one being injured. Hazel didn't know how to label the powers of the mother and child duo, but she was certainly in awe of them.

Bella smoothed her hands across the hem of her jean dress. "I think I'm here to warn you."

Hazel's heart became heavy, sinking into her stomach. "Warn me about what?"

"Rise and shine, doll." Hazel swatted at her nose as she opened her eyes. It felt like a bug was fluttering across her face, but it turned out to be excessively long crimson hair in her nose instead. She sputtered when a lock of Candy's hair fell into her mouth as well. "Get up, doll. You're getting married!"

Icy hands pulled at Hazel's arms, trying unsuccessfully to forcibly get her out of the bed. "Alright. Alright. I'm getting up." Hazel threw the blankets off and climbed out of the bed. "Where's Tate?" She looked around the suite for her fiancé, but all she saw was her fabulously dressed spirit best friend. Thoughts of what Bella told her fled from her mind at the realization that she would be Mrs. Hazel Cormier by the end of the day. She was going to marry the man of her dreams and she couldn't be more ready.

Candy floated near Hazel's classic simple wedding dress, clearly impatient for her to put it on. "He went to get ready in the other suite. It's bad luck for him to see you before the wedding."

Glancing sidelong at her, Hazel pulled her night-shirt over her head. "Candy, he saw me this morning. This is Vegas, so we aren't exactly going the traditional route."

Candy swatted at her as she reached for the dress. "Hazel, you're not putting on this dress until you take a shower. Come on now. Chop chop!" Chilly hands pushed Hazel's bare back as she hurried toward the bathroom.

After having a proper shower and shave, putting on her dress, and having her hair and makeup designed by none other than Candy Townsend, the pair left the hotel room suite and headed downstairs to the lobby. A hundred butterflies took flight in Hazel's chest as she and Candy rode in the elevator to meet Tate. In a traditional wedding, she and Tate would have met at the altar. But this was Vegas, so they would meet in the lobby and head to the chapel together. When the elevator doors opened to the intricately designed circular room, the sight of her future husband took her breath away.

They'd known each other for well over five years, ever since they'd been in undergraduate school in New Orleans. She had been smitten with him ever since, although they'd never dated. Not until less than a year ago. In all that time, Hazel had never seen Tate in a tuxedo.

As a New Orleans police officer, he spent most of his days as a man in uniform, a look that nearly brought Hazel to her knees. When not working, Tate typically dressed just as casual as every other Cajun man. But Tate in a tux was mouthwatering, with his six-foot-plus frame, bright blue eyes, and always slightly messy dark brown hair. He reached out a hand to her as she stepped onto the marble floor.

She beamed at him, still slightly scared he would wake up and realize she wasn't good enough for him. To her surprise, it had never happened, and he smiled just as broadly at her as she smiled at him. Pulling her into his arms, he nuzzled her neck. "You look absolutely beautiful." He kissed her before pulling away to look at her face. "Are you excited?"

She could just barely make out Candy and Jake behind Tate's muscular form. Her best friend was bouncing with excitement as Jake watched her with heart-shaped eyes.

Standing on the tips of her toes, Hazel wrapped her arms around Tate's neck and kissed him again. The touch of his lips against hers always sent a tinge of electricity through her body. "I'm very excited. Shall we go?"

With an ear-to-ear smile, Tate wrapped his arm around her waist and led her out onto the sidewalk as their two ghost companions followed closely behind.

The sky was still bright, the streets flooded with tourists, but Hazel paid no mind to them. She was about to get married, something she'd never seen for herself, but now wanted more than anything, because she was marrying Tate. So, although Bella's mysterious warning hovered somewhere in her subconscious mind, she pushed it as far back as she could. Spirits had caused so many challenges in their lives, but although Bella wasn't a spirit, she would not allow Bella to destroy her wedding day, either.

The chapel wasn't all that far from the hotel, but it was far enough of a walk that Hazel was glad she had opted for flats, not that she could walk in heels, anyway. She glanced back at her best friend who trailed behind them, walking hand in hand with her own man, wearing three-inch stilettos, although no one could see her but Hazel and Jake. Candy blew her a kiss as they arrived just outside the place where she would enter as a single woman and leave as a married one.

The tiny chapel was charming, albeit a bit intimidating. Hazel wanted to marry Tate more than anything, but it didn't make it any less anxiety-inducing to be going through such a tremendous change in her life.

Tate never let go of her as they signed the paperwork and stood in front of the woman who performed the brief ceremony. When they kissed after saying "I do" over the cheering from Candy that only Hazel could hear, they kissed as husband and wife, and it was the greatest feeling in the world.

CHAPTER FIVE

Call in the Night

"How do you feel?" Tate's smile had not fallen even once since they'd left the chapel and made their way to the fanciest restaurant Hazel had ever been to. The server filled their champagne flutes before setting the rest of the bottle in an ice bucket and walking away to put in their order.

"I feel like I'm ready to get my husband back into our bed." Hazel shocked herself at how sultry her voice was, and Tate noticed. His hand slid onto her thigh as he leaned forward and kissed her. For that moment, the entire room disappeared, even the ghostly couple who floated near their table as though they were there to eat dinner as well.

"Are you sure y'all don't want to get the food to go?" Candy shrugged and traced a finger up Jake's ear. Hazel tried to not look too hard at her since it appeared, at least to everyone else, as though no one was sitting there. "That's what I would do."

Hazel gazed into Tate's eyes as she responded. "You and Jake are welcome to go back to your room, Candy. I doubt we'll be out for very long, either."

Candy seemed to need no more encouragement. With an icy kiss to Hazel's cheek, Jake and her best friend floated away from the table before disappearing into thin air. Tate watched her with a smirk, sipping his drink. He'd gotten good at remaining quiet when he realized she and Candy were conversing. Hazel sighed. "And then they were two."

Chuckling, he squeezed her thigh. "So, do you want to get the food to go, then?"

Hazel pursed her lips, very conscious of the hand on her leg. "Tempting, but we have all night, so why not enjoy the experience of being here?" Leaning in closer, she spoke directly into his ear.

"And once we return to the suite, I don't think we'll be leaving again for a while."

When she leaned back in her seat, she could tell by the bulge in Tate's pants just how much her words, or the feel of her breath on his ear, affected him, and it filled her with satisfaction. She'd never felt particularly sexy before being with Tate, and although she still wasn't fully comfortable in her own skin, knowing how much she turned him on certainly helped her confidence.

It didn't take long for Hazel to change her mind and for their food to end up in boxes so they could take their date night back to the suite. She wasn't fond of being out in public as it was, so Tate didn't have to twist her arm all that hard. All it took was a few more touches to her thigh and she couldn't get out of the restaurant fast enough, arm in arm with her new husband.

By the time they got all the way back to their suite, after an extremely public display of affection in the elevator, their food no longer mattered. The boxes were tossed on the hotel room's table without another thought as Tate dropped his jacket on the chair and pulled Hazel close, sliding his fingers into her hair and slanting his mouth over hers.

"Thank you for marrying me." His words were low and breathy as he pulled away from their kiss for only a moment, unbuttoning his white shirt. "I love you."

Hazel yanked at his belt, leaning in to kiss him again, taking his bottom lip into her mouth and nipping it gently. "I love you, too. And I'm still surprised you wanted to marry me."

She let go of him long enough to turn her back to him. "Here, get my buttons."

Slinging his shirt on top of his jacket that hung from the chair, Tate tugged on Hazel's dress, making quick work of the buttons. As soon as he was finished, the sleeves slid off her shoulders before the dress hit the ground, pooling at her feet. No sooner had her dress been on the floor did Tate lower her onto the bed, crawling over her like a predator stalking his prey.

"Hopefully, after today, you'll no longer worry about whether you're good enough." Settling between her thighs, Tate ground himself against her as he trailed kisses down her throat and onto her chest. "You've always been enough, Hazel." His hands slid up her arms, pinning them against the pillow over her head. She panted against him, nearly coming out of her skin with desire. "And even when you've been a handful..." He ground against her again. His hardness was so close to where she wanted him that she moaned. "You were still everything I ever wanted."

The sound of Tate's phone ringing woke Hazel before she'd even fully fallen asleep after they'd made love. The night had been perfect. He always seemed to make her life better, and she couldn't believe they were now married. He would be hers forever. She still pinched herself, hoping she wouldn't wake up from the dream of being his. Even that seemed too good to be true. She was still trying to figure out who could be calling him in the middle of the night when she heard his sleepy voice answer the phone.

"Hello?" Tate cleared his throat while Hazel glanced at the alarm clock on the side table. It was 2:27 A.M.

"Oh. Hey, Sandi. Yeah. Oh, no. Okay... Let me get her."

Hazel was already sitting up in the bed, reaching for the phone, when Tate turned to her. "Mom? What's wrong?"

CHAPTER SIX
The Premonition

Although Hazel had always been close to her mother, since they shared the same gift to aid the dead that passed down the maternal line of her family, she and her parents had become distant over the many years since she'd moved to New Orleans. Her parents had a complicated relationship because of her mother's abilities, and Hazel's relationship with her father had been affected as well. She and her mother had only recently reconnected after years of being estranged, and the relief of having her mother back in her life was palpable.

Working with the dead, as she and her mother were forced to do, had the tendency to take over their lives. Spirits in need did not always respect the boundaries Hazel tried to put up for herself to keep her sanity, and her mother dealt with the same. The lack of boundaries, on top of the often-perilous situations spirits put them in, had caused a significant strain in her parents' marriage. It was the main reason she'd always kept Tate at arm's length, even though she wanted him so badly. She'd rather have kept him as a friend than pursue a relationship that would eventually push him away once she became too much trouble.

Her intentions of keeping Tate as only a friend and nothing more failed when she'd helped an insistent spirit named Angela and had gotten mixed up with the serial killer Raymond Waters. She'd always tried to work with spirits on her own, aside from the help she received from Candy, but the case of Angela's disappearance and murder had become too complicated for her to handle alone. Especially once Raymond had abducted her. She'd needed Tate's help, and although she wanted so badly to keep her secret from him indefinitely, she was forced to expose herself and hope he'd believe her, hope he wouldn't run from her and never look back.

As she should have already expected, after years of friendship with him, he believed her, and he stayed by her side. Actually, Tate learning the truth about her had brought them closer. There was no longer a reason for her to keep him at a distance, so their relationship was able to go where it needed to go. Little did she know he'd wanted her as much as she'd wanted him. So, after over six years of friendship, and only six months of a romantic relationship, they were married, sharing a home, and planning for their future. But the excitement of that all came to a halt when Hazel heard the worry in her mother's voice.

A sniffle came through the phone before her mother spoke. "Hazel," Sandi hesitated. "Hazel, your father had a heart attack."

Hazel's heart turned into a gaping pit in her chest. She hadn't seen her father in over five years and hadn't spoken to him in nearly as long. Suddenly, every reason for the distance seemed insignificant and foolish. The regret threatened to consume her. "Mom...is he okay?" Hazel had a tendency to swirl down into the deepest ravages of her mind and she worried it would happen again if her father was dead.

Her mother cleared her throat. "No, Hazel, but he's not doing well. He's in the Intensive Care Unit. I know you just got married, but if you wanted to see him..." Sandi's voice hitched, and she sniffled again. "It would be good for you to come see him...just in case something happens. Just in case he doesn't make it."

Tate's eyes were wide as he watched her, waiting for her to tell him what she needed. How he could help. She knew, with little doubt, that he would abandon their honeymoon at the drop of a hat if that's what she wanted. Hazel returned her attention to the phone call and her mother, who needed her, needed whatever support her children could provide.

"We'll leave soon, Mom. I'll get the hospital information when we get to New Mexico."

After ending the phone call with her mother, everything moved quickly. They packed their belongings, grabbed their ghostly friends from the suite next door, and took a taxi back to the airport. The vortex that was Hazel's mind threatened to pull her into an endless downward spiral, but Tate and Candy knew to expect it and hovered over her like two overprotective parents. They weren't going to let her be sucked under, not again, and she appreciated it.

Their flight wasn't for two hours, but Hazel couldn't handle sitting in the hotel room any longer, which was why they ended up in the airport terminal so long before their flight. Her muscles felt fidgety, her mind too busy. She had an unwavering need to flee, to run down the road and never stop until the pressures against her eased.

She sat curled into the crook of Tate's shoulder as he ran his fingers through her hair, giving her something to focus on, driving her into the sleep she so desperately needed.

Hazel blinked rapidly, the darkness surrounding her making it difficult to get her bearings. A jolt nearly flung her from where she sat, and she gripped the armrests of the seat until she was white knuckled to hold herself in place. The lights along the floor flared out in the darkness. She was back on the plane.

"Hazel...are you okay?" The tiny voice next to her sent a shiver across her body, raising the hairs on her arms. Sitting in the far reaches of her mind, somewhere between sleep and wake-

fulness, or somewhere else altogether, sat Bella. The child's words before they were separated last time came back to her. It was a warning.

"Bella..." Hazel drifted off as the plane shook again, forcing the trays in front of their seats to fall open. "What was the warning? You said you were here to warn me."

Bella's tiny face looked contemplative as the plane rocked again, affecting Hazel more than it affected her. When the turbulence stopped, the child's eyes bored into Hazel's, burrowing into her very soul. "The plane," the child said, leaving their stare to scan the plane as though she were looking for someone. "They aren't going to make it."

A gasp ripped from Hazel's throat as she woke, choking back air like there wasn't enough. She bolted upright, her eyes wide with terror as the airport terminal came into focus. Tate gripped her shoulders, watching her as though he were unsure how to respond.

"Tate! The plane's going to crash!" Her voice came out frantic and much louder than she'd intended, grabbing the attention of everyone within hearing distance. The nearest security guard took a step closer but halted as Tate searched her face.

"Hazel, what's going on?" Candy and Jake moved in closer, Candy sitting on the other side of Hazel and placing an icy hand on her shoulder.

"Bella... She came to me again... She's been coming to me for a while."

"Emily's daughter?" Candy interrupted, hovering just within Hazel's line of sight. Hazel nodded rapidly.

"I think she was trying to warn me about the flight. We can't get on the plane. Tate, it's not safe."

Tate glanced over his shoulder at the ever-encroaching security guard and the wide eyes of the other passengers seated in the terminal. He pulled her in, tucking her head beneath his chin and caressing her back. "Shh. It's going to be okay, Hazel. You're under a lot of stress. Maybe that's all it is."

Tears had begun to fall down Hazel's cheeks as her desperation grew. It wasn't the stress. It was a warning. Tate rarely seconded guess her and it only made more tears sting behind her eyes. Maybe it was because they were in such a highly charged environment, but she really needed him to believe her. She shook her head and pulled away, her eyes pleading as they met his. Something in her face made his own features soften. He wasn't used to seeing her tears, and it wasn't in her nature to cry for no reason. He glanced over his shoulder again before lowering his face to her level. "What do you want to do?"

The question troubled her. She hadn't gotten that far in her own mind yet. Realizing they couldn't tell the security to ground the flight because it was going to crash made Hazel feel completely helpless. She had no power to stop the flight, but she knew one thing. They were not stepping foot into that jetway.

Swallowing hard, Hazel glanced toward the boarding area and shuddered. "I'm not getting on that plane."

Chapter Seven
Lights in the Darkness

After Tate did a bit of smoothing things over with the airport staff, explaining his wife's fears and nothing else, so as not to make them suspicious of Hazel, they left the airport via a rental car and set off for Santa Fe. They wouldn't get their money back for the flight, but Hazel didn't care. Tate didn't seem to either.

It would take over nine hours to get to the hospital where her father was being treated, and that was one part of the situation that troubled her. She realized she could lose her opportunity to see him while he still lived, and that was heartbreaking, but she couldn't bring herself to get on the plane, even if it would have been quicker. Not after what she'd experienced in the dark space with Bella.

The topography looked the same as they traversed the barren land between Nevada and New Mexico. After leaving in the middle of the night, they were both exhausted, and although Hazel would have loved to drift off to sleep, it was up to her to keep Tate awake, and it was up to Candy and Jake to keep Hazel awake. Thankfully, spirits didn't need sleep. So, Candy made it her personal aim to be the comedic relief Hazel needed. It really was unfortunate Tate couldn't see the chatty redhead, because she was hysterical more often than not.

After several stops for coffee, their rental car crossed the state line from Arizona to New Mexico after over ten hours. Tate's years as a police officer, sitting in his police cruiser and patrolling for hours at a time, had trained him for so much time behind the wheel. So, although Hazel was delirious with exhaustion and felt like she could no longer lift her limbs, he still had at least most of his faculties as they traveled.

Hazel spoke to her mother briefly as they made their way to Santa Fe. After hearing that her father was in stable condition, she and Tate opted to rent a hotel room near the hospital and get a few hours of sleep instead of going straight to the hospital. Her relationship with her mother was newly rekindled, and she wanted to be there for her, but Hazel had a strained relationship with her father. His heart attack had brought her back to her hometown for the first time in a long time, but it didn't make approaching him any easier, even after all that time, even if he was ill. She planned to see him in the hospital. She *would* see him in the hospital. But she wasn't ready just yet, at least not until she had rested enough to have her head in a better place. When they made it up to the joint rooms they'd reserved for themselves and their ghostly companions, the pair fell asleep as soon as their heads hit the pillow.

Mist swirled and coiled around the trees that encroached on the cracked surface of the road. It dispersed as she walked through, but she didn't know where she was supposed to go. It was so dark. Quiet. Eerie. The foreboding sense of a predator was so palpable that not even the insects dared to make much noise. What was she doing there? *She looked around, the smell of verbena and pine on the dry breeze, seeing nothing but darkness. Wrapping her arms around her chest, she rubbed her hands against her skin, more for comfort than for warmth.* How had she gotten there? *Her mind was as dark as the night surrounding her.*

Lights in the distance drew her attention from the landscape back to the road. Maybe she'd gotten there by car. Maybe her car had run out of gas or she'd gotten into an accident and didn't remember. Locking her eyes on the headlights heading toward her, she set off in the car's direction, hoping someone could help her.

Her feet were silent as her shoes hit the hard surface, almost as though she were a ghost, weightless in her form as she moved through space. She moved without real purpose, no understanding of where she needed to go aside from needing to be in the light.

The lights got larger as the vehicle approached her, sending her heart at a rapid pace. Whether it was from fear or excitement, she didn't know, but she was desperate to get out of the darkness. She was too exposed where she was. With her arms outstretched, she waited for the vehicle to get close enough to see her. But just as it was only a few yards away, it was enveloped in an opaque darkness, and the world disappeared.

A warm, callused hand ran across Hazel's back, gently waking her from a welcomed nightmare.

Nightmares had always traumatized her. But, after so many nights in the darkened plane with the living child who shouldn't have been able to be there, Hazel greeted the nightmare with open arms, no matter how unsettling it was. At least, from what she remembered, it had nothing to do with a spirit infestation in her brain, and everything to do with the long drive they'd just traveled and the stress of the situation weighing down on her. Her mind was not the best place to be at the moment, not that it ever was.

"Good morning." Tate's warm smile was only inches from her face. His dark brown hair was sleep-tousled, and he was just starting to get a five o'clock shadow on his cheeks, which made him look even sexier.

"Morning to you." Hazel reached for him, sliding her arm around his waist. She just needed to touch him, needed him to cement her to the present. When the walls were crumbling around her, Tate's presence in her life was the one solid thing she could always depend on. And at that moment, she needed him more than ever. She hated always being so needy.

"Any more dreams of Bella?"

"Thankfully, no. Just a good ole nightmare."

Tate grinned at her and pulled her against his chest, tucking her head under his chin. "Leave it to you to be grateful for a nightmare." He kissed her on the forehead as his hand rubbed her back, making her feel more cherished than she probably deserved. "What am I going to do with you?"

"Hopefully, lots of really good things."

Tate's responding chuckle warmed her in places she needed it, but it also drew in their nosy neighbor. Floating in, already dressed to start her day in a floral sundress, Candy looked radiant. "Are y'all decent in here? Everything covered?"

Candy's hands were covering her eyes, but Hazel wasn't even sure if the hands in front of the eyes trick actually worked on spirits. She was also still not sure how Candy had an unlimited wardrobe in her afterlife when Hazel hadn't bought a new outfit in six months. Leaving her boyfriend behind in their own room, since he was at least respectful of their privacy, Candy crossed into the room and sat in a chair by the window.

Hazel rolled over to face her, putting her back against Tate's muscular chest. "Yes, Candy. We are decent." Pulling her hands away from her eyes, Candy beamed. "But it would be decent of you to not barge in just because you hear us talking. You truly are like a toddler."

Just like a toddler, her beaming smile dropped into a pout. "I'm sorry, doll. I'll try to do better. I'm just excited to see Sandi." Candy looked toward the wall as Jake poked through. It amazed Hazel how much better Jake had gotten at holding onto his energy. When he'd first been murdered, his spirit would fade in and out unexpectedly and out of his control. It was something Candy had been helping him with over the past several months.

Candy was the strongest spirit Hazel had ever met. She'd mastered being a ghost in the few years since she'd been murdered and could do so many more things than Hazel had ever thought was possible. It was a bit unnerving to her and reminded her to never get on the redhead's bad side.

Hazel wasn't surprised at how badly Candy wanted to see her mother. When Sandi had flown to New Orleans to reconnect with Hazel a few months prior and helped her with a case, she and Candy had gotten super close. Especially since Sandi ended up staying in Candy's bedroom. Since Sandi could also communicate with spirits, Candy had been overjoyed to have a new person to talk to, and the two had often teamed up against Hazel. They were quite annoying together, although Hazel realized her mother's mood would be nothing like it had been during the New Orleans visit. Not with her father in the hospital.

"I tell her not to barge in all the time, but you know she doesn't listen." Candy rolled her eyes as her boyfriend approached her, sitting on the arm of her chair.

It no longer phased Tate when Hazel ignored him to communicate with the dead. After living with Candy in his home for months, he'd grown accustomed to it. He often grabbed the gist of the conversation by hearing only one side but knew Hazel would often pass on any pertinent information he couldn't hear.

Tate kissed her head and moved to get out of the bed. "Do you want to take a shower so we can head to the hospital?"

If Hazel was truly honest with herself, the answer was no, an inflexible no, but that wasn't an acceptable answer. So, although she wanted to stay in bed with him and ignore reality, she kicked the ghost couple out of their room and followed Tate into the bathroom.

Chapter Eight
Long Awaited Reunion

Tate had never been to New Mexico, so Hazel truly hated that his first trip to her hometown was under such circumstances. Being from a place of swamps and flat land, Tate took in every detail of the landscape on their short drive to the hospital. Hazel hoped they would have at least a little time to get out in nature before they headed back to Louisiana. Maybe she would be able to show him around her parents' ranch or the state park. She knew he would enjoy any adventure she brought him on that didn't involve ghosts. With that thought in mind, she promised herself not to tell him about the spirits in the state park's campground–or the Native American spirits on the ranch. Ghosts always had a way of spoiling the mood, all but Candy and Jake, and even that exception was iffy.

Parked outside the doors of the expansive rust-colored brick hospital, the spirits that could be found in nature were the least of Hazel's concerns. It would be the lost souls of the hospital that would have been more likely to follow Hazel around, even following her home, begging her for help. With her father in the Intensive Care Unit, and the pressing family dynamic, she didn't think she could add spirit obligations to her shoulders. Not that the spirits ever cared. More than anything, she didn't want her father's spirit on her shoulders. She shut that thought down as soon as it flitted through her mind, which was clearly her own worst enemy.

"Hazel?" She turned to see Tate watching her, an expectant look on his face.

"Huh?"

"I asked if you were ready to go in." He reached out to touch her hand. "I think you may have been in your head again. Do you need more time?"

Hazel took one more assessing look at the hospital entrance, watching a few people walk in and out of the glass doors. The hospital was framed by vast mountains that stretched as far as she could see. It was so unnatural to have a hospital there, such a stark contrast having the man-made structure that saw so much death randomly dropped in the middle of such a beautiful place of nature. She let out a slow breath.

"No use sitting in the car. Nothing's gonna change if I wait to go in."

Tate nodded, leaning over to kiss her before pulling the keys out of the ignition and taking her hand again.

"No matter what happens, love, just know that I'll be there for you."

He didn't even have to say it, although she appreciated it. After everything they'd been through, she knew Tate would always be there for her. So, although worst-case scenarios plagued her in one corner of her consciousness, she swallowed them down and got out of the car.

The day was overcast, as it usually was in Santa Fe. Clouds hung low in the sky, blotting out the late morning sun. Unlike Louisiana, the humidity in the air was low, something Hazel was thankful for as she smoothed her hand over her long ponytail. Instead of humidity, a steady wind blew across the parking lot, not enough to whip the trees, but enough to scatter pieces of litter on the ground. They walked into the hospital hand in hand, with Candy and Jake following behind. Knowing Hazel was holding her breath and struggling to face her father again, Candy was unusually quiet. Whether her father was unconscious, or if he was awake and greeted her with a smile, it still felt like too much.

Being one of the larger hospitals in the city, the lobby was teeming with people, both staff and visitors. Hazel approached the receptionist, getting directions to where her father was being kept, and receiving passes to venture further into the hospital. Biting her fingernails, a bad habit during the times when she was the most stressed, Hazel followed Tate as they made their way to the Intensive Care Unit. When they finally arrived in the ICU's lobby, Hazel's breaths faltered when she saw the man who sat in one of the chairs, a man with her eyes.

"Jason?"

Hazel hadn't seen her older brother since he'd left for law school, more than six years prior, but she would recognize him anywhere. Sitting alone in the corner of the waiting room, reading a novel with one ankle perched over the other knee, her brother looked just like her, just like their father. Jason's hazel eyes lifted from the book in his lap and recognition flared in them. Slinging his book down on the empty seat next to him, Jason rose from his chair and darted toward her.

"Hazel! Oh, my god! It's been forever." Warm arms wrapped around her, squeezing her tightly and lifting her off the ground. "Everyone's going to be so excited to see you." The backs of Hazel's eyes burned as she took in her brother's scent.

Even being at the hospital, her attorney brother was still dressed in a gray suit, the jacket laying on the empty chair next to where he'd been sitting. The top of his white dress shirt was unbuttoned, his striped tie hanging loosely around his neck. He set her back down on the ground and pulled away, beaming.

"Your brother is pretty hot." Hazel and Jake both stared at Candy as she twirled a lock of her crimson hair on a finger. Ignoring her as best as she could, Hazel turned her attention back to her brother. There was no sign of Sandi in the waiting room, or her oldest brother, Terry.

"Where's Mom?"

Jason glanced toward the ICU entrance and then back to her. "She's in the room with Dad. I just needed to get out of there for a little while. The beeping of the machines admittedly set my teeth on edge."

Jason stepped toward Tate with his hand extended, introducing himself before sending their mother a text that Hazel had arrived. The entire moment seemed surreal to her. It wasn't a scenario she could have imagined, all of them seeing each other again after so many years, and in a hospital waiting room. Well, at least she had hoped not to reconnect under such circumstances.

Hazel's mother came out of the ICU a short time later, taking Hazel into her arms. She could tell by merely looking at her mother that Sandi hadn't been getting much sleep. The heavy bags and dark circles under her eyes couldn't lie. After a long hug, Sandi pulled away from Hazel to search her face before hugging her again.

"You look under-slept, Hazel." Letting go of Hazel, Sandi wrapped her arms around Tate's, patting him on his back. "You should let my wonderful new son-in-law take you to get more rest."

"I don't look nearly as tired as you do, Mom."

Sandi scoffed as she left Tate's embrace and approached Candy, who beamed at her. Candy was never close to her own family. They hadn't even bothered to empty her apartment after she'd been murdered. So, although Candy had only met Hazel's mother once, she had become attached to her like the mother she'd never had.

"Well, aren't you a sight for sore eyes," Sandi said as she looked over the redheaded spirit's appearance. "And Jake... good to see you again. I hope you're keeping my girl in line?" Jake grinned and nodded, placing his hand on the small of Candy's back.

Rubbing the back of her hand across her forehead, Sandi let out a deep sigh. "You're right, Hazel. I definitely need more rest." Her mother took a few steps toward the wall and dropped into one of the waiting room chairs. "It's nearly impossible to sleep in the ICU with all the equipment noises and the staff talking."

Jason moved to sit next to his mother as Hazel took the chair on her other side.

"How is he?" It was a question Hazel was afraid to ask, and no answer could have decreased the nervousness filling her. Part of her realized she was being ridiculous. Even if their relationship had been estranged, her father still loved her. If only it was easier for her to pump the breaks on the drama, wouldn't her life be easier?

Sandi's eyes were glossy as she looked at her daughter, taking Hazel's hand. "He's stable for now. They're keeping him asleep and allowing his heart to recover. I keep staying around, just in case he wakes up, but I think I'll go home to sleep tonight—or maybe I'll stay in a nearby hotel. I'd hate to be all the way at the ranch if something happens and I need to get here quickly."

"We can rent a room for you at the same hotel we're staying in." Tate stepped closer and placed his hand on Hazel's shoulder. She couldn't have adored him more than she did at that moment. "It's just a few blocks away." When Sandi glanced up at her son-in-law, her smile met her eyes and she nodded before turning back to look at Hazel.

"Do you want me to take you to see your dad?"

CHAPTER NINE

Why Am I Here?

The sterile scent hit Hazel before she and her mother had even made it through the automatic doors, and the cacophony of the machines tangled with hushed voices made her head spin. What made her even more uncomfortable were the inaudible whispers of the spirits that intermingled with those of the living. She kept her face down as she walked, watching each step of her sneakers as they tracked one step in front of the other.

"No wonder you're so exhausted, Mom." Hazel kept her voice low as they traversed the halls, not wanting to be overheard by spirit or staff.

Her mother cleared her throat. "Yeah. It can get overwhelming at times, but the spirits have left me alone, mostly."

Although she knew the ward was full of those who remained after their lives had ended, Hazel didn't dare raise her eyes. All it took was one moment of notice and she may have ended up with a spirit attachment like a pet she didn't quite want but couldn't get rid of. It was bad enough that she couldn't exactly hide from them. Even if she didn't look them in the eyes, most spirits could sense her and her mother's abilities, so it was only a matter of time before one of them tried to force themselves into her life.

Turning the corner to a long stretch of patient rooms, their steps slowed as they approached one room on the left that had a nurse sitting behind a rolling computer station just outside its window. The nurse nodded at Sandi as they made their way through the partially opened door and into the semi-dark room.

Although Hazel tried to avoid it, the sight on the bed was impossible for her to ignore. The man lying there, covered in tubes and wires, hooked up to noisy machines, looked nothing like the no-nonsense attorney who'd intimidated her for her entire life. He had never been a cruel father. He just wasn't a particularly loving father, either.

Hazel's heart sat barely suspended in her chest, too scared to beat as she hesitantly approached the bed, not wanting to get close, but unable to turn away. Her mother stood back, knowing the moment was charged, knowing how fragile her daughter's resolve was. Any sudden movement and Hazel may have fled like an animal caught in the headlights, so time moved slowly as she watched her unconscious father.

She wasn't sure how long she'd been standing there, staring at the rise and fall of her father's chest, when the room exploded into chaos.

The machines connected to her father's sleeping form erupted into a symphony of sounds as the temperature of the room dropped. Her knees hit the floor, pulling her into the darkness.

"You're back." Bella's tiny voice drew Hazel's attention to the side. The little girl still sat next to her on the plane, but her clothing had changed. This time, she wore a baby blue romper with embroidered flowers down the front. Little white sandals wrapped around her swinging feet.

"Bella." Hazel's voice was choked as she tried to ground herself at the moment. "Why am I here? Why are you here?" Turbulence threw Hazel forward in her seat, pulling a scream from her lungs. "Why do you keep bringing me here?"

The child giggled, playing with one of her pigtails. "I didn't bring you here, silly. You brought me here."

For the first time, frustration filled Hazel, tightening her chest and lacing her words. "Why would I bring us here, Bella? I don't even know where we are."

Glancing around the darkened space, Bella shrugged. "Neither do I, Hazel. Is this not a place you like to visit?"

Hazel scanned the same darkness but didn't see what the child seemed to see. Her heart roared in her chest, the feeling of fight or flight at an urgent level inside her. She rubbed her eyes, making tiny white spots flutter across her vision, leaving only the same obscure blackness in its wake. "No, Bella. This is not a place of mine."

"Hmm." Tipping her head to the side, Bella looked around their seats and into the aisle. Hazel followed her line of sight but still saw nothing. Even the light strips down the aisle had dimmed. "Maybe we're here to help them?"

As though on cue, the lights of the plane came on, illuminating a cabin now full of people. Men, women, and children filled the seats. A baby's cry pierced the air. The knot in Hazel's chest tightened until she could barely breathe.

Where did these people come from?

Violent turbulence hit the plane, sending luggage onto the floor, and screams through the air, before the lights went out again, losing her within the darkness.

A damp cloth slid across Hazel's forehead as she laid against a hard surface. Her eyes were heavy. She left them closed for a while, taking in the familiar male scent surrounding her. It was her favorite scent in the world. *Tate.*

"I think she's coming back." Candy's voice, with all its Cajun charm, floated into Hazel's sleepy mind.

"Wake up, doll." Icy fingers threaded through her hair, a familiar sensation. She loved when Candy played with her hair, although Tate had taken over the job since they'd become romantically involved. Tate continued to pass the wet cloth across her face, not aware of Candy's ministrations.

"Did I fall asleep?" She already knew the answer, or at least she thought she did. Everything was still fuzzy.

Tate's blue-gray eyes stared down at her, worry etched on his handsome face. "You fainted, love. Stay laying for now. Don't push yourself."

Fainted?

Candy, Jake, Jason, and her mother all watched her expectantly, but she didn't know what to say to them. She was just as confused about what happened to her as they were.

Bella's mother, Emily, had the power to pull Hazel into unconsciousness if she wanted to show her something, but Bella wasn't dead. The child wasn't a spirit, and Hazel didn't understand the significance of the plane. She'd been convinced the plane that was going to crash was the flight she was to take the night before, but there hadn't been a plane crash. If Bella was warning her of a plane crash, it hadn't happened yet. That meant she had more time, but she knew nothing else to help her. She couldn't prevent a crash if she didn't even know where the plane was flying to, or from, or even *when*.

Although still a bit lightheaded, Hazel lifted her head from Tate's lap, sitting upright in her chair. "I must just be tired." She knew it was a lie. Sure, she was tired, but that wasn't why she'd lost consciousness.

Everyone but her brother looked at her with equally disbelieving stares. They knew, as well as she did, that her fainting was spirit-induced, or at least psychically induced. Turning to her mother, she refused to explain out loud, not in front of her brother. He knew of her gifts, but he appreciated them just as much as her father did. "Did something happen to Dad? When I fainted, I mean. I heard the machines going off."

Confusion spanned her mother's face as she lowered to the chair next to Hazel, taking her hand. "Nothing happened to your dad, Hazel. There was no change with him or the machines. You just fell into unconsciousness next to the bed."

CHAPTER TEN
Face of a Demon

She and Tate left the hospital as soon as her head cleared, picking up dinner from a fast-food restaurant and returning to the hotel. Her mother remained behind, but only until Jason went to the ranch to retrieve some of his mother's belongings for her hotel room stay. He and Terry intended to stay at the hospital overnight, taking turns while their mother got some much-needed rest. Tate rented a room for Sandi, just as he said he would, leaving the key with the front desk before he and Hazel returned to their own suite.

Hazel was drained from her ordeal with Bella and still had more questions than answers. Once they were alone, she told Tate everything, and hated how his face fell into worry with every word.

"So, there are no identifying factors in the vision that can help you figure out more about the flight?" he asked, tucking her hair behind her ear. "Remember how Celeste told you to keep your eyes open for clues and jot them down? Maybe you should keep a journal of these visions. Maybe that'll help you discover more about the flight."

Tate was right, of course. His head was more organized than Hazel's could ever be. The elderly Wicca woman in New Orleans, Celeste, had proven to be a helpful ally in Hazel's spirit-led ventures, even if her methods were sometimes strange. Hazel grabbed the small notepad and pen from the table next to the bed.

"You're right. The plane is always dark, though. I can't usually see all that much, but I'll jot down what I can and hope to see more if it happens again. Until then, do you think Detective Bourgeois can help us? Maybe he can check with Bella's father and make sure she's okay." Hazel shrugged and scribbled the pen in a circle to make sure it still had ink. "I don't know what I expect from him. I just don't know what else to do."

Tate kissed her on the cheek before grabbing his cell. "I'll text the detective, but don't worry. I know it's hard for you to see this stuff and feel so helpless, but you can't be held responsible for all of it. Maybe Bella does have powers, and maybe she is warning you of a crash, but that doesn't mean if a plane crashes that it's your fault. It's not. You and I won't be taking a plane anytime soon. That I can promise you. But, otherwise, we can only do so much."

Hazel nodded, but she couldn't help but to feel the weight of her visions on her shoulders. There had to be a reason why Bella was showing her those things, even if she didn't understand them. She jotted down what she could, which wasn't all that much. The flight was at night, at least she thought it was, based on the darkness inside the cabin. She guessed at the passenger count, and the color of the seats, which she remembered were blue. It wasn't much, but it was all she had. When she set the notepad back on the table, she felt defeated and helpless.

Tate flipped through the television channels as they leaned against the headboard. With Candy and Jake remaining at Sandi's side to keep her company, the hotel room was quiet. Too quiet. Settling on the local news, Tate wrapped his arm around her shoulder and pulled her into the crook of his arm. She closed her eyes, using the sounds of the television to fill the empty spaces in her mind where unpleasant thoughts threatened to take over.

"A ghostly sighting down Highway 63 has one Santa Fe resident sleeping with the lights on tonight. If you aren't easily scared, the account of what happened to one local resident, Alma, may just change that," said a female reporter on the television, the developing news story pulling Hazel's attention to the screen. The fact that she'd had a dream of a woman wandering down a deserted road the night before wasn't lost on her. The screen changed, zooming in on the figure of a woman whose face was blurred as she recounted her harrowing tale.

"I was on the way to my friend's house late last night, driving down Highway 63. Just out of the city, I approached one intersection that is several miles down the highway when a woman in a white dress stepped onto the highway directly in front of my car. I screamed and slammed on my brakes so I wouldn't hit her." The woman's voice trembled as she explained the events. She wasn't lying. Tate raised the television's volume. "I looked around for her as my car stopped. Out of nowhere, she appeared outside the window of my car, staring at me. She had the face of a demon. It was twisted with red, glowing eyes, and short, pointed teeth. I was terrified. Oh god, I was terrified. She rushed to my window and drug her claws across the glass. I couldn't stop screaming and slammed my foot down on the accelerator. I tried to speed away, but she kept up with me, racing my car and slamming her fists into the window."

The woman paused, lifting her hands to cup her cheeks. Hazel could see the placement of the woman's hands but couldn't make out her features with the blur.

"I didn't know what to do. When she finally did fall behind the car, I saw her in the rearview mirror. She grew taller and taller until she appeared to be the same height as the trees. She was surrounded by a dark mist. She pointed her long finger at me, mouthing words I couldn't make out. I kept driving. I'll never drive that road during the night again. It's cursed."

When the interview ended, Tate muted the television and turned to face Hazel, waiting for her to respond to what they'd seen. First the plane and now a demon stalking the back roads... she swallowed thickly, her chest filling with an overwhelming sense of doom.

"I saw it." Hazel's voice was low and hesitant, almost as though she didn't want Tate to hear. Turning to face him, he searched her eyes.

"You saw what?" She raised her eyes to meet his.

"The nightmare I had last night...I saw a woman walking down an empty road...but *I* was the woman. At least I saw the scene through her eyes. A car did approach, but the vision went black. I didn't see the rest of what that witness said, though. I didn't see red flashing lights or chase the car. I didn't grow twenty feet tall." Hazel glanced at her hands that were laying in her lap. *No claws.*

Lifting her chin with his thumb and forefinger, Tate dipped his face to look at her. "I know what you're thinking, and you need to stop. It wasn't you that the woman in the car saw. It's just a coincidence, and the woman was probably just imagining it, anyway. You have enough on your plate. This story..." He pointed toward the TV, which was still muted. "This story, whatever it is, is not your obligation to solve."

Although not totally convinced, Hazel nodded. She appreciated how much he tried to shield her from herself, and from those entities who threatened to take everything she was capable of giving, even if it dragged her down. He read her like a book, but never seemed to tire of the issues that came up repeatedly.

Flipping off the television and tossing the remote onto the bedside table, Tate pulled Hazel down onto the bed, sliding alongside her. His eyes bore into her as his fingers traced up her side. The nightclothes she wore weren't sexy. They were nothing more than an oversized t-shirt and boxer shorts, but Tate's heavy-lidded gaze looked at her as though she was the sexiest woman in the world. They said nothing for several moments, just listened to each other breathe as she admired the curves of his muscled chest. He hadn't put a shirt on after his shower, leaving his perfect body on display for her.

She bit her lip. "I think we need a vacation."

Tate chuckled, the sound warm and gravelly. "After all this with your dad, we'll try a vacation again. Maybe we'll even leave the ghosts behind."

Hazel huffed, running her hand down his chest. "I don't think it's possible to leave Candy behind. She can be quite persistent."

Warm breath fanned across her face as Tate leaned in to kiss her, his lips lingering, stealing her breath. "We need to let her know it's not negotiable."

Another kiss, this time to the cheek. "She'll understand."

His lips trailed down the curve of her throat, stopping just at the neckline of her shirt. Hazel arched beneath him as he slid his body on top of hers, pulling her top off and flinging it to the floor.

"Candy has her own love life. Even if we enjoy her company, she doesn't need to be a third wheel."

Hazel heard him, but she was no longer listening as his hands and his delicious mouth explored her. Her mind always had a way of distracting her from the best things in her life. Well, her mind and the spirits. She knew she needed to stop allowing everything to distract her from him. He was the most important thing in her life, and she couldn't lose him. The living needed to be a priority over the dead.

Running her fingers through his hair as he kissed the planes of her stomach, Hazel closed her eyes and luxuriated in the moment. There was so much she could say, but she didn't. She let him worship her body as she worshiped his, gave into the temptation of setting all her worries and obligations aside so all there was in that moment was him and her. Tate's body against hers, inside hers, sharing pleasure with him that was solely for them. Morning was sure to bring more challenges, but those challenges wouldn't be in her marriage. That, at least, was the one thing in life she could count on to always be strong and uncomplicated.

CHAPTER ELEVEN
The Urban Legend

Images flashed like flares in the darkness, disappearing too quickly to absorb what they were. Her eyes opened to a lonely scene. Nothing was familiar. She wasn't where she was supposed to be, but where she was supposed to be was also a mystery.

The road stretched in four directions, a crossroads of darkness with no sign of which way to go. Closing her eyes, she cycled a deep breath. How did she get here? With a mental roll of the dice, she turned on her heel and began walking toward the brightest light in the sky. A sense of belonging drove her movements forward while fear threatened to hold her in place.

The trees and mountains stood sentinel as she traveled toward the beacon. It beckoned her forward, but no matter how long she walked, it never seemed to get any closer. Her skin prickled with awareness. She wasn't alone.

The figures were shadows in the darkness, following her as she moved toward the light. Men, women, and children all walking toward the same destination. There were dozens of them, some overtaking her, but none interacting with her, as though they were all on their own journey, arrows barreling toward their targets, shot at different moments in time but traveling along the same path.

The energy surrounding her was heavy, making her feet leaden, each step more difficult than the last. A pit opened in her chest as the light split in two, flickering as it approached. It wasn't any grand quest she was on; it was a vehicle. Why was she here again? Where was she going? *She still didn't know the answers, but she kept moving forward.*

Waving her hands in front of her face, she stepped to the side of the road. Even if it wasn't a light that would transport her to a better place, maybe it could at least bring her home. But as soon as the lights came within only yards from her, they were enveloped in a black cloud.

She was alone again. Nothing was familiar.

Jolting upright, Hazel gripped the bed, feeling the solid surface beneath her, the warm body next to her. The person in her dream had been so confused, so lost in the darkness. It took a moment to realize she wasn't that person. She wasn't lost. She was in the hotel with her husband, who she touched to make sure was really there. Loosening a breath, Hazel laid back down on the bed, curling into Tate's side. He still slept, but his arm snaked around her, pulling her in close.

Eventually, after staring at the shadowed ceiling for a while, Hazel fell into a dreamless sleep.

"I need to go to that highway." Hazel didn't know what she would find there, but she was seeing that highway for a reason. Tate's eyebrows furrowed.

"You really think there's something to the story from the news?"

She shrugged, taking another sip of her coffee and grimacing. After so many days of room service, everything was starting to taste the same and none of it was good. "It could be nothing. But between seeing it on the news, and having dreams about it, I can't ignore it."

Candy, Jake, and Hazel's mother sat in the small living room of their suite, chatting about everything under the sun. If anything could lift Sandi's spirits, it was Candy. Hazel looked over her shoulder at them before turning back to the mirror and pulling her hair into a ponytail. Rinsing his toothbrush, Tate turned to face her.

"When do you want to go?" Hazel hadn't gotten that far in her plan yet. It was always an internal battle when deciding what spirits to help and which ones to ignore. Even if ignoring them was damn near impossible.

"We should probably go tonight, although I'm not exactly excited about it."

"Go where?" Candy called out from the sofa. Moving to the seating area and sitting next to her mom, Hazel went into an explanation of what they'd seen on the news as well as what she'd seen in her dreams.

"Sounds like La Mala Hora," Sandi said, a light of recognition flaring in her eyes. Jake, on the other hand, looked like he may be sick. Sweat beaded on his ghostly face as his eyes grew wide. Even being a spirit himself, he still wasn't used to the creep factor of the paranormal world. Candy, however, appeared ready for an adventure. It wasn't surprising.

"La what?" The red-haired spirit sat with her feet tucked below her, more like floating, but her movements usually mimicked that of a living woman. Sandi reached over and patted Candy's shoulder. Although a spirit, she appeared solid to Hazel and her mother. Her form was icy, but there was often a mass to her that they could feel, even if the rest of the world couldn't.

"La Mala Hora," Sandi repeated. "It's an urban legend here in New Mexico, although I believe it came from Mexico originally. It's said to be a bad omen. People will see it down dark roadways, usually near a crossroads. They say it appears as a black mass at first, but then turns into a woman as it gets closer. It's said to signify impending death."

The hair on Hazel's arms stood on end, chilling her very blood. "Even after all I've seen, that sounds terrifying. Do you think it's real?" Hazel clinched her teeth while waiting for her mother's response, hoping for one answer but expecting another.

"I hope not," Candy chimed in. Tate sat on one of the chairs at the table, leaning over with his elbows on his knees, waiting for Sandi's response as well. Hazel couldn't imagine what he was thinking, but she knew the last thing he'd want was for her to get involved with anything like what her mother was describing.

"I don't know if it's real, but I know there are definitely believers out there."

They left the hotel for the hospital a short time later. Although Hazel's mother knew a little about the phenomenon described in the television interview, it didn't settle Hazel's need to see it for herself. It wasn't going to stop those visions from crowding her dreams. The visions never stopped until she acknowledged the cause of them and found a way to settle the spirit. Although she wanted to ignore it, she couldn't.

A sleeping man was the only person in the ICU waiting room when they arrived. Curled up across a row of seats with his arm beneath his head, Hazel didn't recognize him, but her mother did.

"Terry," Sandi said as she crossed the room, laying a hand on Hazel's oldest brother's shoulder. Terry shifted, rubbing his hands across his eyes before sitting up. Unlike Hazel and her brother Jason, Terry looked a lot like their mother. His light brown hair was disheveled from sleeping in such an awkward position, and his clothes were wrinkled. Terry, like Jason, was an attorney, but he was also a new father, so she wasn't surprised by his sleepiness. Blinking several times, he jumped up from his seat and darted across the waiting room, pulling Hazel into his arms.

"It's so good to see you," he said as he gripped her hard enough to squeeze the breath from her lungs. Hazel had never been a very affectionate person, at least not with anyone other than Tate, so her brothers' responses to her return continued to take her by surprise. If they missed her so much, she didn't understand why they'd never come to see her in New Orleans. She wasn't the only one who could buy a plane ticket, after all. Even with the discomfort she felt, she pushed those reservations aside. This reunion meant a lot to her mom. So, although part of Hazel wanted to pull away, she allowed the hug to continue, patting her oldest brother on the back.

"Good to see you, too." When her brother pulled away to shake Tate's hand, it took a conscious effort to set her face into something more pleasant than what she felt.

They all took a seat in the waiting room as Terry caught them up on how Hazel's father had done overnight and what the hospital's plans were for the day. To everyone's relief, he was still stable and improving. The doctors intended to ease off his sedation throughout the day, waking him to see how his heart fared. It sounded as though her father would recover, even if he needed medication for the rest of his life to keep his blood pressure and cholesterol under control.

Sandi exhaled as she rose to her feet. "I'm going to go in and speak to the nurse. Hazel..." She looked at her daughter. "Do you want to try to go back in?"

Tate sat forward in his chair, gripping Hazel's hand, and she knew why. After what had happened the day before, after she fell unconscious in her father's hospital room, neither of them felt comfortable with her going back in. Sandi's lips became a thin line as she looked at each of them and nodded. "Let me check with the nurse and see if an extra person can come back. Would that make you feel more comfortable?"

The question was aimed at Hazel, but she looked to Tate for the answer. They shared a glance, Tate's hand squeezing hers gently, before Hazel responded. "I'd rather Tate be in there, just in case I pass out again."

"Say no more," was all Sandi said before disappearing behind the double doors.

Hazel's mother was only gone for a few minutes before returning to the waiting room to take her and Tate back to her father's room. In a way, Hazel had hoped the hospital would stick to their rule of only two visitors at once, but she guessed it was best for her to face him again. She needed to grow up. She knew that. There were so many complex feelings inside her she still didn't understand, but she needed to unpack them. Maybe that would be the positive side of this entire situation. Maybe her family would be able to get past the walls that had separated them for so long and become a family once again. Being in the same room as her father would be a start in mending that wound.

The air in the Intensive Care Unit was heavy, but Hazel didn't know if it was because of the thoughts weighing her down, or the spiritual presences within the ward. Unlike the previous day, when the spirits of the ICU paid Hazel and her mother little attention, a night of charged energy had made the mother and daughter incredibly popular. Spirits seemed to crawl out of the woodwork, peering through open doorways and under counters, spirits of every age and gender. Holding onto Tate's hand until she was white knuckled, she tried to keep her head down. If she ignored them, maybe they'd leave her alone. At least that was her mantra, even if it rarely turned out to be true.

They took the turn down the hall of her father's room, with Candy and Jake following behind, only walking a few steps before their path was blocked. Tate, ignorant to the female spirit in their way, proceeded to walk through her, provoking ire in the spirit's face. Of course, it didn't work. The woman, appearing to be around Sandi's age, huffed loudly before following them down the hall.

"Hey!" The woman shrieked as she pursued them, flying ahead and standing in front of Hazel again before she maneuvered around the persistent spirit once more. Tate glanced at her with a curious look on his face, a look that usually made her blush, but she only mouthed the word 'spirit' and continued to watch her feet as she walked.

"Hey, to you!" Candy responded, throwing her arm over the female spirit's shoulders, the latter shooting her an incredulous look and skirting away. Jake laughed, but Candy, never one to be ignored, followed the spirit, chasing her down the hall and away from their group.

Seated on the small sofa near the window, Hazel sat next to Tate and watched as the medical staff turned back the dial on her dad's sedation. Candy returned from dealing with the ghost, who'd had the same tenacity as she had, a short time after chasing her down the hall, and now hovered with Jake by the window. According to Candy, the spirit was angry about her ex-husband's new wife staying at his bedside. Apparently, there was nothing like the wrath of a jealous woman, even after death.

Sandi sat in the chair closest to her husband's bed, holding his hand as he slept peacefully. The sounds of the machines in the surrounding rooms played like an orchestra of the unwell, drawing Hazel's attention away from her own thoughts. They seemed to sit there for hours, waiting for something to happen that never did. Her dad stirred, but he didn't wake. By the time Hazel and Tate left the hospital that afternoon, Sandi was still waiting.

CHAPTER TWELVE
Swirling Blackness

The moon was merely a tiny sliver as they made their way to the highway where the La Mala Hora sighting had taken place. Since Hazel was admittedly a terrible driver, Tate sat behind the wheel of their rental car, although he did not know how to get where they were going. Unwilling to be left out of absolutely anything, Candy and Jake sat in the backseat of the car, even if Jake was scared out of his wits and had no interest in joining in the night's activities. Hazel found it endearing just how uncomfortable he was with the paranormal and appreciated his presence all the more.

The heaviness of dread hummed through her chest as she watched the lights of the city fade in the rearview mirror, her body knowing there was more to the story than what she hoped to find. Her homecoming to New Mexico had been such a long time coming, but she never expected to find herself tangled in an urban legend mystery when she did return. It made her want to turn around and head straight back to New Orleans. Not that one of the most haunted cities in the country provided a reprieve from such things. If anything, her life had been more plagued by the supernatural in New Orleans than it had for the first nineteen years of her life. Loosening a breath, she reached over and took Tate's hand. He grounded her, no matter where she was, and she needed him at that moment.

There weren't many cars on the road as they turned onto Highway 63, heading in the direction of the state park. The area already gave Hazel the creeps, even without the added sighting of La Mala Hora. The local Holy Ghost State Park was known for its spirits, including the infamous killer priest, which was one of the many reasons why Hazel had stayed far away from the area, aside from the fact that she was not an outdoorsy girl. She'd hoped to change that with Tate and show him the beautiful sights Santa Fe offered, but La Mala Hora was ruining that for her.

The air chilled as they approached one of the several crossroads on the darkened highway. She shuddered, glancing toward the backseat where her best friend gazed out of the window.

"Are you okay?" Tate asked as he squeezed her hand gently. "Do you feel anything?"

Hazel shrugged as she looked out of the window. Trying to make sense of the wild, darkened landscape was impossible. If there were an evil presence out there, it would have to climb onto her lap before she noticed it. "Nothing I don't usually feel. It's just creepy out here."

"You can say that again," Jake added from the backseat. Candy cooed at him, cuddling into his side and kissing him on the cheek. Hazel giggled, wishing, as she always did, that Tate could interact with their friends.

"Jake agrees," she said. Tate smirked and glanced in the rearview mirror. He couldn't see their friends, but it never stopped him from acknowledging them, which they appreciated as much as Hazel did.

She watched the darkened miles pass, the trees accented by the occasional shadow of a house or structure. There was no longer an expectation of anything out of the ordinary to appear, or at least she hoped not. People imagined supernatural experiences all the time. Even if Hazel knew such things were real, that didn't mean all those claims were factual. Tate drove the car at a steady speed, his years as a police officer training him to be a cautious driver, even on the twisting mountain road.

Hazel was about to tell him to turn around when a swirling darkness loomed ahead of them, chilling the air in the vehicle.

"Tate..." Trying to keep her voice calm, she turned to face her husband. "I don't know if you see that, but stay calm, and slow down."

Tate wasn't known for losing his cool, so Hazel's instructions for him to remain calm were more for her sake than for his. He knew that as well as she did, but he slowed their speed and held the wheel with both hands, waiting for further instructions. She watched the black mass as they approached, hoping it was her imagination even as she realized it wasn't. They'd found La Mala Hora.

The blackness swirled in the beam of their headlights, spreading and warping as though it was a liquid suspended midair.

"What in the hell is that thing?" Candy, no longer distracted by the nearness of her lover, leaned over in between Hazel and Tate, staring out the front windshield.

Hazel ran her hand across her forehead, fear building in her chest. "I don't know. Tate, pull over here."

Still not seeming to see what she saw, Tate scanned their surroundings before doing as she asked, placing the car in park as far away from the road as he could. "Do you see something, love? It's not safe to sit on the side of the road at night like this."

She knew he was right, but she needed to get to the bottom of this entity on the road. She needed to understand what connection it had to her, if any.

An icy hand prevented her from getting out of the car, even as she reached for the door handle.

"No way, doll. You don't know what that thing is. No way I'm going to let you get out of the car." Candy's beautiful, carefree face hardened into a more serious expression than Hazel was used to. Tate watched her, oblivious to the interaction she was having with her best friend, but his face revealing his own worry.

When Hazel turned back to look at the mass in front of them, it was gone. She should have felt relieved, but instead, the knot in her chest tightened. Her questions wouldn't get answered without understanding why she was seeing this highway in her dreams, even if it scared the shit out of her. Sighing, she turned to face Tate. "It's gone. We can head back to the hotel."

Candy relaxed back into the back seat as Tate nodded and scanned the empty highway before placing the car back into drive. It only took a moment before the nearing object caught her attention, bright light emanating from the swirling black mass as it barreled toward their car.

"Tate, watch out!"

"Hazel! You're back again!" Bella's usual pig-tails were replaced by a single ponytail as she sat in the blue cabin seat at the back of the plane. Hazel swayed on her feet as she held onto the backs of two seats, standing a few feet away from the little girl. "I was coloring while I waited for you. Do you want to know what I was coloring?"

Putting one foot in front of the other, Hazel made her way to the seat next to Bella and sat down. "Bella..." Hazel had a difficult time hiding her exasperation. The darkness wasn't Bella's fault, or at least she didn't see how it could be.

"What am I doing here? How are you doing this?"

The incredulous look Bella gave her was older than her age. Straightening the hem of her white dress, Bella sighed. "I already told you I'm not doing anything, silly. I was just sitting in my bedroom, drawing a picture of a lady in a white dress, and then here I am...sitting here with you."

Leaning over, Hazel clasped her head in her hands. Her head pounded as she tried to understand what had been happening, before she found herself in the darkness with Bella again. The realization hit her like a knife to her chest. The wreck.

Tate!

"Bella! I've got to get back to my real life. It's urgent. Something's happened to my husband!" Holding onto her head, Hazel's breaths came in short bursts. Something was wrong. "How do I get back?"

Jolting up onto shaky legs, she scanned the plane before slumping back into the seat. There was nowhere she could run to get back to him. She had to wake up. Bella watched her outburst but didn't offer any guidance.

"I don't know what you mean, Hazel. I don't know how to get back home either. One minute I'm there, and the next minute, I'm here."

Bella was having the same experience as she was, which offered her nothing to go by, nothing to help her get back to Tate. Her heart squeezed painfully. She had to get back to him. Rising from her seat again, Hazel only made it one step before falling back down. Her head swam. It pounded. Dropping her head into her hands again, she could no longer fight her tears as the first sobs exploded out of her.

The temperature of the plane dropped as she cried, ice cracking across the small windows, drawing lines across the panes like spiderwebs. Bella's breathing vanished, throwing Hazel into an eerie silence. Dragging her palms across her eyes, Hazel dared to look up, squinting into the darkness.

Liquid blackness swirled in front of her, warping and shifting like ink filling the air. The hair on the back of her neck stood on end, but she couldn't look away, almost like she was being compelled. She watched in stunned silence as the mass pulsed, its shape rippling as it molded itself into something familiar.

Her eyes didn't dare to blink as the entity floated toward her, becoming tall and slender until it nearly reached the ceiling of the plane. She swallowed, her heart beating loudly in her ears.

A flicker of light shined in the darkness, blasting it apart, leaving nothing behind but the figure of a woman. A woman in a white dress. Her face was unrecognizable. The woman stepped toward Hazel as the plane shook, reaching out and touching Hazel on the cheek before everything went black.

The world spun into focus as Hazel's eyes opened to the flashing lights of a police car. Tate cradled her in his arms, wrapped in a blanket as their rental car was cranked onto the back of a tow truck.

"Tate?" The hand rubbing her arm halted as he heard his name on her breath. It was barely more than a whisper.

"Shh." Tate resumed rubbing her arm as he spoke into her ear. "Everything's okay."

Candy and Jake hovered nearby, watching her as they waited in the back of an ambulance. The paramedics moved around her as they readied to leave the scene.

"What happened?" She tried to sit up, but the throbbing in her head forced her back down against his chest. He wrapped his arm around her, discouraging her from trying to sit up again.

"A car driving without their headlights on hit us as I was getting back onto the road. Everyone's okay though. Don't worry."

Not worrying wasn't in Hazel's DNA. Through the lights of the emergency vehicles, she could just make out the red sedan parked on the opposite side of the road, the driver speaking to a police officer who looked to be about to administer a test for intoxication. Her eyes squeezed shut as another throb hit her head.

"How will we get back to the hotel?"

Getting back to the hotel was only one of the many worries that hit her mind. There was also the issue of the rental car, and whether she had a concussion. The paramedics, seeming to trust in Tate's own emergency training, watched her, but didn't intend to take her to the hospital, something Hazel was thankful for.

Tate sensed her growing list of worries and squeezed her against him, kissing her cheek. "I told you not to worry. I called your mom to let her know what happened and the tow truck driver will give us a ride back to the hotel. We'll be able to get another rental. I'm more worried about whether you're okay." Pulling away just enough to look at her, his eyebrows lowered as he scanned her face. "You passed out again, but I don't think you hit your head. I didn't see any marks on you. I admit, however, that your fainting came at an inopportune time. If you hadn't woken up soon, I was going to send you with the paramedics." Worry creased his face as he pulled her into him again. "Was it another vision?"

"Yes." He lifted her in a bridal hold as the ambulance prepared to leave the scene. Although perfectly capable of walking, Hazel enjoyed him holding her too much to protest. Moving toward the tow truck, Tate set her down onto the passenger seat, while the driver finished chaining their rental car in place. "I was back on the plane." She hesitated, scanning the darkness surrounding the road, but not seeing anything aside from Candy and Jake floating nearby. "But I saw that entity. I saw La Mala Hora."

CHAPTER THIRTEEN
Waking the Sleeping

It seemed to take an eternity for them to arrive back at their hotel. By the time they pulled into the parking lot, Candy and Jake had already disappeared to wherever spirits went when their energy waned, and Hazel and Tate could barely keep their eyes open. They trudged to their suite as the night threatened to vanish into day, falling onto their bed without changing into their pajamas.

Needing sleep more than they needed anything else, they slept until nearly noon. Her voicemail was filled with worried messages from her mother, but Hazel was in no rush to do much of anything. After washing their night off in the shower and ordering a pizza, she finally sat down and returned her mother's calls, making no excuses for the fact that they intended to remain at the hotel for the day. Her head still pounded, and she couldn't handle much more on her exhausted shoulders than what she'd already dealt with in the past few days. Thankfully, Sandi understood.

Just as they were about to lie down for a late afternoon nap, another message came through to Hazel's phone, but this one was only a text. All her mother said was, "Your father is awake."

Hazel stared at the screen for a while, numbness filling her where she knew other emotions should be. It wasn't that she wasn't happy. Of course, she was glad her father was going to be okay. It was just that, after being absent from her life for so long, he was virtually a stranger, so her heart didn't know how to process the feelings she should have. Tate held her as she stared at the screen, wrapped around her back like the big spoon he was. He never pushed her to process her emotions, or to react quicker than she comfortably could. His patience was one of the many positive attributes that made him much too good for her, even if he denied it.

Forcing herself to come up with a response, she texted back to her mother, saying that it was great news, before setting her phone aside and curling back into Tate's chest.

"Have you changed your mind about going back to the hospital?" His question caught her off guard, mostly because she didn't have an answer. Instead of responding, she shrugged. "Whatever decision you make is perfectly acceptable, love. After last night, you need a day of no obligations, no matter what's going on in the world."

Even if he was a million times too good for her, he truly was exactly the person she needed to settle her. Where Candy revved her up, rarely accepting a single excuse, Tate allowed her to just be, bringing her peace when she needed it. She required both of them in her life, both sides of the coin, but she needed him at the moment she found herself in.

Taking his hand in hers, she draped his arm across her stomach. "I may change my mind later. But, at least for now, I don't want to rush to the hospital. I'm exhausted, mentally and physically. Plus,

I doubt seeing me right away would be good for easing him out of days of being unconscious."

Tate's warm breath fanned across her neck as he moved in to kiss her. If anyone could distract her from the looming stressors in her life, it was him. Leaning into his touch, she closed her eyes, willing the darkness behind her lids to enhance the moment, and not send her into the downward spiral that was her mind.

Tate's muscular arms wrapped around her as he deepened the kiss, his tongue as luxurious as his bare skin against her. Her husband really was a delicious man, and he in his police uniform really was a chef's kiss. Jealousy always threatened to consume her anytime she saw another woman eyeing him too hard, even if that person was a little old lady who needed help to cross the street. Candy and Jake's stalker killer's obsession with him only mere months prior didn't help one bit. Thankfully, Harmony went to prison, and Tate's shoulder had fully healed from the bullet wound the killer had given him.

Hazel met the swipes of Tate's tongue stroke for stroke, the dance of their bodies perfecting from all their time spent together. Never one to seek out a man's affection, her love for Tate, after years of being his friend, had changed all that, made her crave him on a level she never knew was possible.

Their touches became feverish as they kissed until there was nothing between their bodies but blistering heat.

"You two really are lazier than the dead." Hazel awoke to blue eyes the size of moons only inches from her face.

"Candy, must you be so damn close?" She swatted at Candy's face as Tate rolled over, blinking up at her. The pink tint of sunset gleamed in through the curtains of their hotel room. They'd slept the entire day away.

It only took a moment for Hazel to realize that, when Tate rolled over, he was utterly naked, and showing absolutely everything. Candy's eyes grew wider as Hazel threw herself over, fumbling with the blankets while she covered him. Tate, still half asleep, didn't register what was happening nearly quickly enough.

"Woah. He's a shower, isn't he?" Dramatically dropping her jaw, Candy flopped onto the sofa, blasting them with an icy breeze. Mortification, mixed with a bit of annoyance, filled Hazel.

"Hush. You shouldn't even be in here."

Tate's cheeks couldn't have turned any redder as he gripped the blankets across his chest. "She *really* shouldn't be in here."

Candy, of course, felt no shame as she watched them, clearly amused at how uncomfortable they were. "Look, I wouldn't be here if Tate's phone hadn't vibrated so hard that it fell clean off the table. I heard it from next door. I guess you two were preoccupied.”

Hazel glared at her best friend's shit-eating grin before wrapping the sheet around herself. Grabbing Tate's cell from the side table, she handed it to him, her eyes never leaving her impish friend. Jake was nowhere to be found. “Where's your boyfriend, Candy? Shouldn't he be keeping a leash on you? Is he 'a shower?'”

Hazel didn't really want to know anything about Jake's cock, but since Candy felt the need to comment on Tate's, it was only fair game. Candy's grin only widened, and she winked before disappearing back through the wall, returning only a moment later with a smirking Jake by the arm. “I told her not to come in here while you guys were sleeping,” he said, eliciting a huff from his girlfriend. They both dropped onto the sofa across the room.

“It's the detective,” Tate said, pulling Hazel's attention from the ghostly couple. “He's looking into the flight. There haven't been any recent crashes, which we've already deduced. Should I tell him to keep an eye on certain flights?”

Scanning the browser on her own cell, she ran through the list of airlines with the same color seats as in her visions. Something in her told her to look at flights flying in and out of Santa Fe, even if there were no indications in her visions to suggest it as a destination or starting point. There was also no reason for her to believe that the La Mala Hora visions, and the plane visions, were connected, but her mind still connected them, anyway. If seeing La Mala Hora was meant to be a bad omen, then maybe it was foreshadowing a plane crash. Maybe it really was connected.

When Tate set his phone back down, Hazel leaned against him, thoughts of her family flooding her mind. She'd gone all the way there because of her father's heart attack, yet she'd slept the day away as soon as his eyes had opened. It wasn't right, and she knew it. She needed to go back to the hospital, no matter how uncomfortable it made her.

Candy, seeming to expect Hazel's next words, grabbed Jake by the hand, pulling him up from the sofa. "Come on, hot stuff. Let's give them some privacy so they can get dressed. We'll head to the hospital."

Hopping off the bed as soon as Candy's red hair disappeared through the wall, Hazel reached for the pair of jeans she'd left draped over the chair. Even though dirty laundry was her arch nemesis, she and Tate would need to visit the hotel's laundry facilities the next day, or she would be spending her days naked. Just the thought of Candy finally catching Tate nude after trying for months made her scowl. Tate watched her from the bed, probably waiting for her to get out of her own head and share her plans with him, but she still wasn't sure of them herself.

"I think I want to go to the hospital." The words sounded surer than she felt, but it didn't stop her from dressing. Climbing from the bed, he placed a kiss on her cheek before heading into the bathroom. When the door opened and he came out fully dressed, Hazel's heartbeat sped up to an uncomfortable pace. After over five years, she was going to see her father.

CHAPTER FOURTEEN
Roughly Constructed Walls

The sun had set by the time Hazel and Tate climbed into an Uber and headed to the hospital. They still needed to get a new rental car, but that was a problem for another day. The night was cool, making her glad she'd grabbed a jacket before they'd left the hotel. Tate, used to living in the stifling South, with no knowledge of New Mexico's chilly nights, had left all his jackets back in New Orleans. She cycled a breath as Tate reached for the hospital's door, scents of the sterile environment hitting her nose, replacing the refreshing aromas of the sage and earth outside.

Deciding to head to the hospital unexpectedly, Hazel hadn't contacted her mother before they arrived, but she expected Candy to have spread the word when she and Jake went to the facility less than an hour before.

By the time they arrived in the waiting room, it was empty, forcing Hazel to text her mother and let her know they were there. Fidgeting and biting on her nails, she lingered near the double doors, too nervous to sit down. Thankfully, it didn't take long for her brother Jason to exit the ICU and come out to greet them.

Her brother looked tired. He'd probably gone to the hospital straight after a day in court or meeting with clients. Although Hazel had left her career as an attorney behind her for the betterment of her sanity, her brothers were still at the height of their own careers. Realizing leaving her career was one more reason for her father to be disappointed in her... No, she would not think about that. Leave it to her mind to bring up her black sheep status before reuniting with the family member who put her there. Clenching her teeth, Hazel nodded to her brother and entered the double doors for the Intensive Care Unit, leaving the security blanket that was Tate back in the waiting room.

Being almost time for visiting hours to be over, the ward was quiet, aside from the near constant beeping of the lifesaving machines and the hushed voices of the medical personnel. No spirits followed Hazel as she made her way down the hall to her father's darkened room, which was a blessing. When she turned the corner and into the open doorway, her feet seemed to stop working, planting her in place at the room's entrance.

Her mother was seated in a chair near the bed, a blanket wrapped around her shoulders, as she spoon-fed soup to the man lying in front of her. Hazel didn't see Candy or Jake anywhere. Her father, Roman, was a shadow of his former self, although she realized she hadn't seen him in so long that she couldn't have known how much of that aging had happened during his brief hospital stay. His dark brown hair had thinned a bit on the top, his face more drawn than she'd remembered. But his eyes, his eyes seemed to light from within when she walked into the room. Her heart raced as she stood just inside the doorway, glancing to her mother who let the spoon rest in the soup bowl, and back to her father who watched her. A hesitant smile spread across Sandi's face as she waited for either father or daughter to speak first. Her father looked at his wife before returning his hazel eyes to his daughter, a genuine smile on his face.

"I would get up to hug you, Hazel, but I'm afraid the wires would yank me right back into this bed."

It only took a moment for her father's words to crack through her roughly constructed walls before Hazel closed the distance between them, wrapping her father in a hug as the first tear fell from her eye. She'd spent so much time away from her family, every year away making the return to them even harder. After a while, her own trepidation had grown into a monster of her own making in her mind. Why would she not be surprised if she'd done it to herself?

Even with the IV in his hand, and the blood pressure cuff on his arm, connecting him to various cords and tubes, Hazel's father rubbed her back as he held onto her. No urgency to let her go. None of how she'd felt in the past mattered anymore. If he could put it behind him, then she could put it behind her. Having her family back was in her grasp, the strings weak and frayed, but she still intended to hold on to them and hope they strengthened under her grip. As long as her mind didn't prevent that from happening.

"I've missed you," Roman said as he pulled away from her just enough to look into her eyes. His hands trembled on her shoulders. Or maybe it was she who trembled. "You look well, Hazel. And I can't wait to meet my new son-in-law. Police officer, is it? That's an admirable position."

Hazel smiled as her father looked at her with an adoration she'd never seen before, or at least not in her short memory. She nodded. "I know he's looking forward to meeting you too." Tate had never mentioned such a thing, but she knew it was true. He was, after all, the nicest guy she'd ever met.

"Do you want me to go and grab him?" Sandi rose from her chair, motioning for Hazel to take her spot next to the bed, and leaving the room before Hazel had a chance to protest. Watching the doorway as her mother disappeared into the silent hallway, Hazel's mind had never felt so full of empty space. Without the support of her mother's presence in the room, she didn't know what to say to the man who lay only a few feet from her, watching her expectantly. Thankfully, her mother was only gone for a few minutes before returning with Tate by her side.

Hazel's reunion with her father had gone better than she'd expected, although it was brief. Visiting hours forced Hazel and Tate out of the room only fifteen minutes after Sandi had brought Tate in. It was good timing, however, because it was clear her father's energy was draining. Even if the visit was relatively uneventful, it was heavy on her emotions, too.

By the time they got up to their hotel room, the shock of the evening had worn off, and the exhaustion of the past twenty-four hours had poured in, along with aches and pains Hazel didn't know she had. There were no visible wounds on her body from the crash, but she was certainly beginning to feel the impact. She grimaced as she pulled off her jacket, draping it over a chair.

"Your dad seems to be doing better." Unbuttoning his shirt, Tate looked exhausted, but he still drew her in. She couldn't help but to wrap her arms around his muscular frame, snuggling against him and soaking in his scent.

"He does seem to be getting better. It's good to see. I know my mom has got to be exhausted."

Tate held her close, his warmth intoxicating. "You're exhausted. And you're hurting. I saw you massaging your neck. It's normal after a crash, no matter how small, but let's get you into the bath so you can soak your muscles. Hopefully, it'll fade by tomorrow."

Hazel nodded, but she didn't make a move toward the bathroom. It felt too good to hold him. "I haven't seen Candy in hours. Maybe I should check their room. It isn't like them to be missing in action for so long."

Chuckling, Tate stroked his hands up her back, eliciting a groan from her. "Your mom probably sent them away. There was enough going on without them lingering. Did you ask your mom if she'd seen them?"

Hazel shook her head. Walking in to see her dad's eyes for the first time in years, she never thought to ask whether her mom had seen her ghost best friend that night. With as much as Tate's words threatened to put her at ease, it was only right for a head of excessively long red hair to slide in through the hotel room wall. No knocking. No warning.

"I know what you're going to say, doll, but my eyes are one hundred percent closed."

Hazel rolled her eyes as she peeled herself away from Tate. "You can uncover them, Candy. We are totally appropriate right now. Unfortunately."

Tate's grin told her how unfortunate it truly was as he left her side and walked into the bathroom, the shower starting only a moment later. When Hazel turned back to look at her best friend, it was with a deep sigh. "Where were you earlier?

As light as air, Candy floated toward the sofa and lowered herself onto it, crossing her legs in the process. The emerald mini dress hugging her petite form was much too sexy for the occasion. "We were going to go to the hospital, but we figured your parents would need their privacy, so we went back to the scene of the crash. Although Jake was a total chicken about it." Candy's big blue eyes flicked to the side as her boyfriend slid into the room, looking incredibly flustered. When her best friend looked back at her, it was with far less humor on her face. "We need to talk."

CHAPTER FIFTEEN
The Drawing

A sinking feeling hit Hazel's chest as she lowered herself into a chair across from Candy and Jake. She couldn't say that Candy was never dramatic, because her best friend was as dramatic as a person could be, but this was different. Or maybe it was Hazel's own emotions making the moment more ominous. Either way, she gripped the seat as she sat, bracing for what the spirit couple had found at the crossroads.

"What is it? What did you see there?" Hazel shifted uncomfortably in her seat. "You're kind of freaking me out."

Jake made a face Hazel couldn't decipher, but Candy responded before she had to ask about it. "We saw her. La Mala Hora. She's real."

Releasing the breath she'd been holding, Hazel slumped in her chair as the bathroom door opened. She only spared Tate, and all his still dripping sexiness, a glance before turning her attention back to Candy. "Any idea what she wants?"

"We didn't get close to her, but she called to us."

"What do you mean she called to you?" The air suddenly seemed thinner than it had been before. Tate approached her from behind, setting a supportive hand on her shoulder. He could only hear one side of the conversation, but she would fill him in later.

Candy smiled at him, even if he couldn't see it, before her face fell back into something more somber. "We could hear her calling us to her, but not with her voice."

"More like we felt compelled," Jake added, the usually laid-back man grimacing.

"Compelled? What was she calling you for? What did she want from you?" Hazel hadn't intended her questions to come out so frantic, but it wouldn't have been her if they hadn't.

Candy shrugged, but Hazel knew there was more. There was always more when it came to the predicaments they found themselves in. "If I had to guess, I'd think she was after souls." Jake moved closer to his girlfriend, putting an arm around her and pulling her against his side. Candy laid her head on his shoulder. "And, Hazel, La Mala Hora isn't a ghost. She isn't like us, if it's even a *she*. I'm not sure what it is."

Ice chilled Hazel's veins as she looked up at Tate, who still held onto her shoulder. Reading something in her face, he pulled her up from her chair and lowered himself into it before pulling her onto his lap. His nearness always did something to soothe her constantly frazzled nerves. Taking a moment away from her conversation with Candy and Jake, she recapped the details to Tate, his face turning grimmer as she went. When Hazel returned her attention to the ghostly couple sitting across from them, she didn't know what to say next. This situation was so far above her head that she couldn't even see it in the clouds. She didn't know how to grasp the meaning of any of it.

"If it's trying to gather souls, no matter what it is, I don't want you or Jake going back out there." It was the first thing that came to Hazel's mind when Jake told her of the compulsion they'd experienced. She couldn't allow that thing to take them away. The thought sickened her, forcing bile to rise in her throat.

Jake would've accepted her demand without question, but Candy was as stubborn as the day was long. She was always up for an argument, or at least a bargain. "I don't want you going back there either, Hazel. I don't know what that thing is, but I think we can all agree it's not good. You got into a damn car crash out there. You or Tate could have gotten really hurt. Or worse. We all need to stay far away from it, whatever *it* is."

That was something they could all agree on. Hazel had no interest in returning to the dark roadway that led to where a paranormal entity acted like a black hole for spirits. She didn't know where spirits went when they left the plane of the living, but she didn't think it was wherever that thing might take them. She hoped Candy was wrong about La Mala Hora's purpose, but they had no way of knowing. Not unless someone dared try to speak to it, and she wasn't volunteering. She didn't think she was.

Candy and Jake left after their conversation ended, both agreeing to stay away from the mysterious entity, yet both knowing the other's guarantee was conditional. Hazel always promised to stay away from danger, but there were always circumstances that drove her right into its arms, and her best friend always came running shortly behind. She thought about it as she rose from Tate's lap and pulled off her clothes, tossing them onto the ever-growing pile of dirty laundry on the floor before heading to the bathroom. The tub had been calling to her since they'd gotten back from their accident and she was done ignoring the need to unwind. At least she could try to.

"We need to do laundry tomorrow. This room is starting to look like my old apartment."

Tate's chuckle made her grin. His head peeked into the bathroom a moment later, scaring her half to death. "Hey... I kind of miss your old apartment, although I do prefer you living with me."

"Even though I brought a needy ghost with me? One who never knocks?"

His smile didn't even falter as he responded, which she knew was genuine. "Even though." Opening the door wider, he stepped further into the bathroom, his large frame taking up most of the small space. "Do you want me to wash your hair?"

Knowing just how much she hated the task, Tate didn't wait for a response before he grabbed a cup from the sink and filled it with water, pouring it over her head as she reclined in the tub. "Did I ever tell you how perfect of a man you are?"

The scent of his skin filled her nose as he leaned forward to kiss her. "Once or twice."

"Mommy said to tell you hi."

If there was ever a statement Hazel didn't want to hear from Bella's tiny lips, that was it. Her heart sank into her gut as she leaned her head back against the seat, the turbulence shaking the craft around her. The little girl's mother had been enough of a handful when she haunted Hazel to last a lifetime.

"You still see your mom?" The question came out hesitant. She didn't really want to know the answer, because she didn't understand how it was possible, and she didn't want Emily haunting her again.

Bella nodded. "I see her sometimes, but not like I see you. She doesn't take me anywhere. She just shows up in my bedroom to tuck me in sometimes." The little girl twirled a lock of her hair that was left down instead of in the usual pigtails. "But mommy can't stay with me, she says. Only for a minute, she says."

Hazel didn't know what to say to that. She didn't even understand how Emily was visiting Bella after she'd already crossed over. Even after her years of helping spirits, she still didn't understand how the whole "afterlife" thing worked. Grimacing, she glanced around the plane. It was dark again. She couldn't see anything, but her body was still on edge. She hoped the woman in white wouldn't step out of a black mass again. The figure may have helped her return to Tate last time, but it still scared her half to death.

"Bella, have you figured out why we keep coming here?"

One shoulder lifting in a shrug, Bella pulled a piece of paper out of her pocket, unfolding it across her lap. Hazel gasped, her blood running cold as she released the grip on her armrest to grab the drawing.

"How do you know this, Bella? Did you see this?"

The image, drawn and colored by the hand of a child, was still unmistakably a picture of a crashed airplane. The trees and mountains framed the drawing, with the wreckage scattered across the road, a highway sign, New Mexico Highway 63, planted firmly in the ground.

CHAPTER SIXTEEN

Insurmountable Challenges

Hazel jolted awake. She had to go back there. That was the only thing on her mind when she woke from the darkness again. Still trembling from the vision, she shook her husband awake. Black sky still dominated outside, the moon merely a sliver cutting through the night when Tate rolled over and opened his eyes.

"Tate... the plane is going to crash on Highway 63! We have to do something."

Tate cupped her cheek, kissing her before searching her face. "Slow down, love. What did you see? What happened?"

Sparing no detail from her vision, Hazel recounted what Bella had said to her before explaining the picture the little girl had drawn. His eyes were wide, his face contemplative, but he didn't interrupt. If Tate wasn't who he was, he would've probably had her committed to a mental health facility for delusions. Still, she always worried when her spirit happenings would tip the scale and become too much for him. He'd always assured her it would never happen, but she'd seen the same problems plague her parent's marriage. She just had to hope that would never happen with her own relationship. Pushing the thought away, she focused on the hand stroking her face, willing it to calm her as it always did.

Tate grabbed his phone, gripping it tightly before turning back to her. "This crash... any sign of when it was going to happen?"

Having no other answers, Hazel shook her head. She needed to return to the darkness, needed to return to the highway, wherever she could find out more. There was only so much she could do with the information she had.

His lips thinning, Tate seemed to think for a moment before he unlocked his phone and began typing a message. "I'm going to text the detective and let him know what you saw. There's no guarantee he'll see this tonight, or that he can do anything about it. Countless flights pass over Santa Fe. There's no way to know which one it'll be, but we can at least pass on what we know."

When he set his phone on the bedside table, pulling her back down onto the bed against him, a little of the urgency left her. "Thank you."

The feel of his firm hands against her skin made her forget the stress of only moments before. "You don't need to thank me, baby, but I do need you to realize that there's only so much you can do. Okay?" His fingers cradled her chin, tipping her eyes up to meet his. "I need you to hear me out. I don't know how or why you're seeing these things, but I don't want you taking this responsibility on yourself. This is too much for one person. I couldn't handle it if you got hurt. I love you too much."

She nodded, wishing it were that easy. "I love you, too. More than anything. And I would shut it off, if I could." Tears burned the backs of her eyes. So many lives depended on her. How could she deny them? But she wasn't qualified to handle any of the things being thrust upon her. The pressure was immense.

There was no hiding the emotion in her eyes. Tate's muscular arms wrapped around her, pulling her against him until they shared breaths. "I know you would, and I'm with you every step of the way. You know that, right?"

She did. Even with the doubt she had in herself, she never had any doubt in him. Not knowing how to express what she wanted to say, she kissed him. Words sometimes failed her, but she could show him how she felt, how much she appreciated him.

Tate kissed her back, his lips hard and soft all at once. At the base of everything else in her life was that raw need they had for each other. It was an undeniable force she could always count on when everything else got too complicated. And this situation, between her father, the seven-year-old living child stalking the darkest places in her mind, and the urban legend turned real life villain, was *complicated.* All she could do in that moment was nothing at all, at least nothing regarding those three insurmountable challenges weighing down on her. All she needed to do was show her husband how much she loved him, and that part was easy.

Hazel hadn't even realized she'd fallen asleep when she woke up to the sun shining in through the hotel room's curtains. When Tate had rolled off her, after worshiping her body until every bit of her had been wrought with pleasure, she had no more energy left to keep her eyes open. He still slept next to her as she gazed at him, his tousled hair making her grin. His eyes didn't remain closed for long under her stare, however, and they were bright when they opened. Stress never seemed to affect him like it affected her. He always took every-thing in stride, and she wished she had that ability to compartmentalize like he did. It was one of the things that made him an excellent police officer and an even better partner in life.

"How long have you been watching me sleep?"

"Not long." She smoothed the hair off his fore-head. His dark brown hair was thick and seemed to grow quicker than should've been normal. Sometimes she wondered if he was secretly Har-ry Potter and giggled to herself. "It's hard not to watch you when you're so handsome when you sleep."

He chuckled, pulling her on top of him in one swift movement, her legs opening to straddle him. "Am I only handsome when I'm asleep?"

Even though she hated it, and always threatened to punch him in the groin, he dug his fingers into her sides and tickled her. Her body jerked as she laughed, hoping she didn't pee on herself. "Stop! Stop!"

His maddening hands stilled at her pleas, pulling her into a bear hug and groaning, the sound bringing back memories of their night together. Traces of him still lingered on her bare skin, just as she liked it. "I'll stop, but only because I love you. And I know you're probably about to pee on me."

Smacking his chest, she stuck out her tongue at him before springing from the bed and running to the bathroom. He knew her too well, and she certainly had to pee. By the time she returned to the bedroom, Tate was already out of the bed and pulling on his jeans. Unlike Hazel, who slept like the dead and woke like a zombie, Tate was unequivocally a morning person. She would never understand such rare and unusual creatures, but she'd tolerate him, since he was perfect otherwise. When he leaned over to scoop up their dirty laundry, she nearly swooned.

"We should probably get this washed, although I wouldn't mind keeping you naked and in bed. Then maybe you'd stay out of trouble."

Hazel smirked as she pulled on her last pair of semi-clean jeans, the pair that had a stain of an unknown origin on the left thigh. She followed behind him as he headed out the door in search of the laundry facilities, knowing he was right about her needing to stay naked to stay out of trouble.

If anything kept her from getting into precarious situations, it was Tate. Candy was the one who was usually around when she got herself into a jam. So, it was no surprise when the familiar mane of fire-red hair crowning the head of a salaciously dressed spirit slid through a doorway, trailing behind them as they stepped into the elevator. Her boyfriend, with his dark-rimmed glasses, held onto her arm.

CHAPTER SEVENTEEN
Let it Go

Thankfully, the laundry facility was empty when the group of four barged in, Tate's arms full of their dirty clothes. Hazel had yet to explain her dream to Candy, not with three strangers riding the elevator with them. Once they closed the door to the room, she didn't have the same reservations.

Hopping onto the top of the dryer, she went into an explanation of what she'd seen in her vision, the humor in Candy's expression falling as she listened.

"So, you're going to go back there?" Candy's tone was incredulous. It hadn't been but a handful of hours since they'd agreed that neither of them would return to the crossroads. Even so, after as long as they'd known each other, it shouldn't have surprised Candy that she would put herself into a hazardous situation. No matter how many times she'd already been in situations sure to be her undoing, Hazel still found herself running toward danger like a kid to a candy store.

"I don't see how I have a choice. I know it's a long shot, but I need to at least try to save those people."

The lid of the washer slammed and then Tate's arms were around her, pulling her against his chest. "We already talked about this. It's not your responsibility to save these people, no matter how much they need to be saved. You're only one person, love. Don't put that pressure on yourself. You know I'll always support you, but I don't like it."

Hazel nodded, letting Tate's strength fill her as her chest tightened. The last thing she wanted was to upset him, but she didn't want dozens of people to die, either. Leaving the washer to clean their clothes, the group left the laundry room and headed back up to their suite.

Sun burning across the sky, there was more calling for Hazel's attention than just the woman in the black mass. She needed to return to the hospital. Her father had only been awake for a day and her mom probably needed support from her kids, even if they were all grown and had their own lives.

When she and Tate returned to their hotel room, Candy and Jake followed. Knowing she intended to go back to the crossroads, she wouldn't be able to get rid of her best friend, even if she wanted to. There was still a problem, however. They didn't have a car. So, before they could return to the hospital, or to the crossroads after sunset, they needed another vehicle.

Leaving shortly after putting their laundry to dry, Hazel, Tate, and their ghostly companions had set off in a rideshare vehicle toward the rental car company. The paperwork for their accident had been extensive, but they were able to leave in another sedan once it was done.

After losing hours while getting another rental car, with as much insurance as they could buy, Hazel was starving, and she had no interest in more food from a drive thru. Stopping at a Mexican restaurant instead, somewhere with food that didn't come from a freezer, the couple sat down for a late lunch.

Candy and Jake had faded out just as they'd parked the car to conserve their energy until their night trip back to the crossroads. Hazel didn't want her best friend, or her best friend's lover, to return to the place where a spirit-seeking entity lay in wait, but she couldn't expect Candy to stay behind. They would be careful, but whatever waited for them down that darkened highway, they would have to face it together.

"I heard back from Detective Bourgeois." Tate set his cellphone down on the table. Hazel hadn't even noticed him pick it up while she was face-first in her veggie burrito. Her stomach dropped.

"What did he say?"

"There wasn't much he could say. He has a contact with the FBI who sometimes uses psychics on cold cases. He agreed to speak with them about your visions, but there isn't a lot to go on. Still, he can at least put the red flag on someone else's radar, someone who has the potential to help."

With some relief after receiving the detective's message, Hazel and Tate made their way back to the hospital. She knew her mother would be there. Even with her parents' hardships, they'd pulled together in her father's hour of need. She appreciated her mother's loyalty, even if her father didn't deserve it. Reuniting with him had smoothed away only part of those hard feelings after years of being estranged. Her walls had cracked slightly when he held her, allowing her to think about putting everything behind them, but a new day had brought doubt with it. She didn't know if she could forget everything she'd felt throughout her life.

The waiting room was empty when they made their way up to the ICU, her brothers undoubtedly with their families, at least Terry probably was. Jason was probably nose-deep in a case file in his office, his second glass of whiskey getting low within his grasp. She couldn't complain. Her brothers had been there for all the years she hadn't, but they also had their own lives.

Texting her mother as they waited on the other side of the double doors, it only took a moment for Sandi to join them. Unlike days in the past, her mother's eyes were brighter, the bags and dark circles less pronounced. As soon as she came through the doors, she pulled Hazel into a hug, all smiles instead of tears.

"Your father is doing so much better today. It sounds like they may send him home tomorrow!" Sandi sounded so happy. Hazel should have been excited too but returning to her family's ranch was one more thing she would have to mentally prepare for. "Will you be able to come to the house with us, help your father settle in? Or do the two of you need to head back to New Orleans?"

Looking back at Tate, Hazel already knew the answer. Tate had offered to take a few extra days off if she needed him to and going back to their home would be the equivalent to her abandoning every person on that damned plane, even if she didn't know how to prevent the crash. Candy and Jake would follow them wherever they went, having no real obligations in their afterlife. Aside from being with each other, they had nowhere else to be. "We can stay for a little longer. I'm still trying to figure out this thing with La Mala Hora."

Taking her hand, Sandi led her to the chair, sitting beside her. "Maybe you should let that one go, Hazel. It's already proven to be dangerous."

Her mother didn't tell her anything she didn't already know, but her mother also didn't know about the plane visions, so Hazel told her everything. Sandi had been there when they'd rescued Bella from her mother's killer in the swamps of Louisiana. She knew the child had otherworldly powers, but she hadn't expected Bella to have the ability to do what she was doing to Hazel's mind. Even Sandi, who'd lived in the paranormal world for much longer than Hazel and had even spent her life learning from her gifted mother, had never heard of such things. Whatever abilities the little girl had, they were something else altogether, something unlike their own. It still raised a question, one that Hazel had no ability to answer anytime soon, and that was what part of her life Bella would continue to play, if any.

Bella may have had abilities Hazel wanted to understand, but the little girl was also only seven-years-old. She was a minor under the care of her father, who would not appreciate Hazel showing up on his doorstep with wild claims. Sure, there was a chance Bella's father knew of his daughter's abilities, but after the interactions Hazel had already had with Joshua, it was unlikely. Not to mention he'd just lost his wife. There was no use in Hazel even trying to communicate with him. So, at least while the little girl was so young, Hazel had to accept that they would only meet up in the dark place between their realities. There was no other choice.

Clearing her throat, Hazel stood. "Should we go back in to see Dad?" Their first visit since his heart attack had been so pleasant, albeit surreal, that she was almost scared to push it further. It was only a matter of time before she did something to make her father express his disappointment in her, especially if the conversation came up about spirits. With the spiritual pressures on her at that very moment, the chances of that happening were likely. Her mom shook her head.

"Not right now. Your dad is asleep, and they'll be moving him to a regular room tonight. He's being taken out of the Intensive Care Unit. You can visit him later this evening, if you have time."

Hazel nodded, unsurprising relief washing over her. She would need to see her father again, if only to relieve her of the walls she had built over so many years, but it wouldn't be at that moment.

CHAPTER EIGHTEEN

Only an Imprint

Their second drive to the crossroads was more ominous than the first. The air in the car was alive with energy, strumming through Hazel and speeding up her heartbeats. They never made it back to the hospital. After the hours spent retrieving a new rental car before they went to the hospital the first time, and the equally extensive time spent cycling through the rest of their dirty laundry, Hazel had little time nor energy to add one more errand on top of their obligations for the day. She had little doubt Bella would stalk her subconscious mind again that night, or perhaps she would see the mysterious spirit walking down the road in her dreams, but she still felt the need to confront the woman in the black mass.

The moon was high in the sky as they rounded the bend in the road and headed down Highway 63. Darkness reigned over the area, the trees looming like silent, all-seeing sentinels. There were very few vehicles traveling the highway, to Hazel's relief.

The closer they got to the sight of their crash, the harder Hazel's heart beat in her chest. Closing her eyes, she tried to center herself as she gripped Tate's hand. Candy and Jake sat in the backseat, remaining on high alert as the car advanced, focusing their energy on feeling for the summoning sensation they'd experienced the night before. If the entity was there, they may have been able to feel it before Hazel could see it. After the events from the last time, they would have to be extra cautious. Above everything else, she needed Tate to remain safe, even if he insisted on protecting her.

When they arrived back at the site of their crash, Tate pulled to the side of the road, leaving the car's emergency lights on in case another car approached them. They didn't want anyone to stop, but they also didn't want to be hit if their car wasn't noticed.

They sat there for a while, everyone on high alert except Tate, or at least he didn't show it. She knew he didn't want to go back there. He'd voiced his concerns before they'd left the hotel, but he understood her reasoning, and he was as supportive of a husband as was possible. Tate's main request through every one of her spirit-led journeys was for her to take him along for the ride. Without him, she had a tendency to get herself into more dangerous situations. She had left him out of things enough for her to know better, so it was something she'd agreed to stop doing once they'd gotten engaged.

Their surroundings were quiet and dark, with no sign of anything supernatural nearby aside from the two spirits in the backseat.

"Maybe it's not here," Candy said, leaning forward between Hazel and Tate. The chill of her closeness made Hazel glad she'd brought a jacket.

"That's what I'm starting to wonder. If she were here, would she not approach us?"

Candy shrugged. "I'd rather it not approach us at all, but I guess we're not going to stop trying to speak to it until it does."

Knowing her best friend was right, Hazel didn't respond. Instead, she scanned the darkened landscape again, squeezing Tate's hand.

"Hazel, look." Candy pointed toward the windshield as a flicker of light moved toward them.

Hazel stared at it, unable to make out what it was from the distance. She reached for the door handle, but Tate tugged at her hand.

"I don't like this, Hazel. It's not safe for you to be out of the car."

Squeezing her eyes shut for a moment, she nodded. "I know, baby, but there's something coming this way and I can't get a good look from here. Candy and Jake need to stay in the car. I don't want the entity pulling them in, if that's what it was trying to do last time. I have to go out there."

Turning off the ignition, Tate reached for his own door handle, pushing the door open. "Then I'm coming with you."

The moon provided a small sliver of light in the darkness, illuminating the reflector lights that ran down the length of the highway. Aside from crickets and the occasional critter, the air was silent. Hazel and Tate walked hand in hand along the shoulder of the road, toward the flickering light that seemed to hover just above the highway, drifting toward them.

Hazel would have thought the figure was a spirit, but the way its light flickered in and out unsettled her. It was a woman, that much was clear, but it wasn't La Mala Hora. Unlike La Mala Hora, who had matted black hair nearly obscuring her face, and a long white gown that drug the ground at her feet, this figure had lighter hair, and wore what looked like jeans and a shirt. Whoever it was, whatever it was, it wasn't La Mala Hora.

"Tate... I'm gonna walk ahead. I see her now, but she'd probably disappear if you got too close." Glancing at him, she found him watching her. "Would it be okay if you waited here for me?"

Tate loosened a breath but nodded. "Stay on the shoulder, far from the road. I'll stay right here, but

I'm running after you if I see anything concerning." Pulling her in for a kiss, he released her hand. "Be careful. Okay?"

"I will."

Touching his face, Hazel smiled before she walked away.

No matter how warm her jacket was, she couldn't stop the chill that seemed to linger in the air, infiltrating her clothing and prickling her skin. She knew it was more because of the eeriness of the place than the temperature, but it didn't make her any warmer. She walked slowly, staring ahead at the spirit, not wanting to scare her. The woman's form blinked in and out like a television with a poor signal, or an overhead fluorescent light that needed a new bulb.

As Hazel got closer to the spirit, it became clear the woman wasn't moving at all. It was like she was walking in place, although it was apparent that she at least thought she was moving. With hesitation, Hazel approached her, still not quite convinced she was a spirit at all. She'd seen hundreds of ghosts over her lifetime, probably even thousands, but she'd never seen one who flickered like that. Also, the spirit didn't even look at her when she approached. It was almost like they were in two separate universes, overlapping but not quite in the same place.

"What's your name?" Something else was curious about the spirit who walked down the road. Unlike other spirits, the surrounding air wasn't icy. It was almost as though she wasn't there at all. Like she was an imprint on the environment. The spirit didn't respond to her. It didn't even look at her.

"Where are you headed? Maybe I can help you find your way?" Hazel glanced back at Tate, who still stood off to the side of the road, watching her but not moving any closer. She owed him big time for being the best husband on the planet. When she looked back to where the spirit was only moments before, she was gone.

CHAPTER NINETEEN
The Plan

The words entered Hazel's mind for the first time, but she had to share them, because even she couldn't believe herself. "I think I should talk to one of those ghost hunter groups, one familiar with the La Mala Hora story." One of Tate's eyebrows arched in that familiar way Hazel loved, but he let her continue. "I know what you're going to say, and I know most of them are total frauds, but I need some help in understanding this thing."

After losing sight of the strange spirit at the crossroads, they'd returned to their hotel room for the night, showering and climbing into bed. With all the uncertainties of the situation, Hazel couldn't sleep. She thought about contacting ghost hunters to see what evidence of the entity they could find, but she was hesitant. She knew many of those groups fabricated their findings, or worse, antagonized the spirits.

"You could probably find a local historian as well. They may not physically look for La Mala Hora, but they're probably well-versed in the story since it's so central to the state. But you should do so in the morning."

Snuggling into his arm, she kissed him. "Your idea is better than mine. We should do that as well."

Tate's responding agreement was no more than a gravelly sound reverberating from down in his chest. It made her toes curl. There was no way he was going to allow her to talk about, or even think about, the situation anymore that night, and she couldn't say she minded.

When Hazel woke the next morning, tucked like a little spoon against Tate's chest, she couldn't help but to feel disappointed. Not because she was in her husband's arms, and not because their night tangled in each other hadn't been amazing, but because she hadn't dreamed the night before, or had even been pulled back into the darkness with Bella. She couldn't get any of the answers she needed if she didn't see those who had them, even if she hated how it felt to be in a situation where she had little control. She felt even more helpless without them.

Although she hated waking to no new answers, when Tate's eyes opened that morning, she greeted him with a genuine smile, laying on her back to look into his eyes. If all else fell apart in the world around her, he would still stand as a pillar against the storm and she would never lose sight of that.

"Good morning." The way he always told her good morning first, with his voice still a little raspy from sleep and his dark hair tousled, turned her on even on the worst mornings.

"Good morning to you. How did you sleep?" Wrapping his muscular arm around her, Tate pulled her into his chest, and she let him, taking in his scent.

She huffed. "I didn't dream or see Bella." Nuzzling into her neck, he kissed her skin, making it difficult to think about anything else. "Usually, I'd be happy about that, but I kind of need answers, so I wish they would have come to me."

Nodding against the curve of her neck, he kissed her skin again. "They're not exactly considerate of your schedule."

She giggled as she moved slightly away from him when his hair tickled her, only for him to pull her closer again. "You're being very distracting this morning, my love."

"Mmm hmm. That's my job. Sometimes I just want your attention all to myself."

His words made guilt grow inside her chest, even if they weren't meant to. "I know, and I feel the same way, even if I've been really distracted lately. When all this is dealt with, we really need time to ourselves, even without Candy."

When he pulled away to look into her face, she could tell by how his eyes softened that he understood. She would make it up to him. *Soon.*

It didn't take them long to get dressed once they'd gotten out of bed, not since they now had clean clothes. Once they were ready, Hazel and Tate left the hotel to go to the local coffee shop, with Candy and Jake in tow. She'd brought her laptop, opening it in front of herself as soon as they'd snagged a table in the corner. She searched for local historians, and a dreaded ghost hunter group, anyone who could help in her quest to understand La Mala Hora.

The local historian, a middle-aged man named Paul Sims, agreed to meet them at the library two hours later. Discussing the entity with anyone other than those closest to her made her nervous, but it would be necessary. Even so, she had no intention of telling the historian about her abilities. She didn't, however, have the same hesitations when speaking to the ghost hunters. The Ghost Patrol, a local group comprising three men and a woman, was more than delighted to meet with her that evening.

Against her better judgment, Hazel admitted to the ghost hunters that she could communicate with the dead. She figured it was the best way to get them to take her seriously and actually meet with her. She also realized she may regret that admission later, but they saw her as one of their own, so she'd hoped it wouldn't be too much of a disaster.

Hearing their number called, Tate went to the counter to get their breakfast while Hazel shut down her laptop, placing it back into her satchel. When he set the food down on the table, she was more than ready to eat.

A text from her mother came in just as she pulled her breakfast sandwich toward her, confirming that her father was getting released from the hospital that afternoon and then her parents were returning to their ranch on the outskirts of the city. She had no intention of going there, at least not that night. Maybe meeting with the ghost hunters was an excuse to skip returning to her parents' home, but she planned to do it anyway.

"I can't believe you're actually going to meet with spirit chasers, doll." Although Candy spoke to her, Hazel kept her eyes on Tate. "They are so *not* your kind of people."

Hazel snorted. "Not many people are *my* kind of people."

Tate laughed at that, biting into his breakfast sandwich.

Tossing her napkin at him, she rolled her eyes. "Hey... what is that supposed to mean?" Candy smirked at him, but he only shrugged and took another large bite of food. It was no secret she wasn't a people person, but she wouldn't allow the opportunity to mock offense to pass her by.

"Are we going to go with y'all tonight? I'd love to see if they can really detect us. It would be a good way to check the effectiveness of their equipment," Jake said. His words were serious, but Hazel couldn't deny the mischievous look on his face. She wondered if he wanted to mess with the ghost hunters. When Candy reiterated the idea, Hazel realized they'd discussed it previously. She didn't put it past her best friend.

"What are the two of you planning? Looks like you're up to no good. I can feel it."

No one had the ability to look as innocent as Candy did. Her giant cerulean eyes made it impossible for her to not have a doe-eyed expression. "I don't know what you're talking about, doll. I am one hundred percent innocent. At all times."

More ridiculous words had never been spoken, but Hazel returned her line of sight to her husband, who was watching the one-sided exchange between his wife and the spirits he couldn't see.

"So, what should we do until we have to be at the library?"

Tate's eyebrows lifted as he sipped his coffee. "You don't want to swing by the hospital?"

There was no way for her to hide the reaction on her face, her lips scrunching of their own accord. "Not today. He's getting discharged and they're heading home. It's too far out of the way with everything going on today, and I really don't feel like being at the hospital before he leaves. I'm sure there's a lot going on."

"That's understandable. Hey." Grabbing her hand, Tate's smile was bright. "Since he's going to be okay, maybe we can get back to New Orleans soon. I bet you're just as ready to go home as I am."

She was more ready to go home than even she realized. Still, with the unsolved case looming over her, she couldn't go home just yet.

CHAPTER TWENTY
Harbinger of Death

The Santa Fe Public Library was a historic building. Built in 1908, it had spirits of its own. Hazel remembered the library, and its spirits, from growing up in the area. Each section of the building seemed to have a mind of its own. Taking in a breath, she and Tate exited the car and headed toward the entrance.

The local historian had a time-worn face, but his eyes were kind, even though they were hidden behind rather thick glasses. It was hard to tell with the gray in his hair, but Hazel figured he was in his fifties, if not older. His clothes were semi professional, a button-down shirt tucked into khaki pants, but they were slightly rumpled. If anything, he had the appearance of a college professor.

"Hazel?" His voice caught her by surprise. She hadn't realized she was probably staring.

Reaching out, she shook his hand. "Yes. Paul, is it?"

He nodded, motioning toward a cluster of tables in the corner of the room. She followed.

Mr. Sims already had a scatter of documents on the table before they'd sat down. It was clear he'd been there for a while. Tate pulled out her chair, pushing it in once she sat down before lowering into his own.

"So, you're interested in the infamous La Mala Hora?"

The amusement in his tone caught her by surprise, but she leaned forward to look at the collection of items before her. "I am."

The documents were nothing official, mostly personal accounts and a few grainy photos. Still, she looked through them before scanning the pictures. Most of the witnesses may have been making their experiences up, or mistaking what they saw, but a few of the pictures certainly looked like what she'd seen at the crossroads, or at least a faded version of it. A familiar sinking feeling hit her stomach as she held onto one of the photos in her hand, dread filling her at seeing the entity again.

"You're welcome to make a copy of anything you need," Mr. Sims said as he pulled his cellphone out of his pocket. Hazel could just barely make out the sound of it vibrating. "There's a copier near the desk. I'll be right back." Answering his phone in a low voice, the historian left through the door and walked out into the parking lot.

Hazel still held onto the picture she'd had in her hand for the past several minutes. The photo was dark, as it always was in the areas where La Mala Hora was said to stalk, but the blurred form in the corner was unmistakable. Part of her wondered if the picture was a fake, but if it was, it was a damn good one, because she'd seen that figure before.

"Is that her?" Tate leaned in, tipping the photo toward himself. Hazel gladly released it in his grasp. She'd looked at it enough.

Loosening a breath, she shuffled through the other documents on the table, pulling out one of the testimonies. "Certainly looks like it. I would think the photo was a fraud, except it's so close to what I've seen with my own eyes."

"She's creepy as hell." Tate set the picture back down on the table and pulled one of the documents toward him, taking a closer look.

"Yeah. I admit she freaks me out a bit, even with everything I've already seen." Unimpressed with the person's claims, she moved on to a different individual's explanation of what they'd experienced. Just as she was about to read what they'd written, Paul Sims returned to their table and sat down.

"Do you have questions about anything, Hazel?"

Looking up to meet his eye, she set the paper in her hand back down. "Can you just give me a rough explanation of what La Mala Hora is and what she's after?"

Nodding, he pulled the stack of documents toward himself and moved his glasses further down on his nose.

"The legend of La Mala Hora spans many regions, including in Mexico, so the accounts differ some.

Some people think it might be a spirit, whereas others think it could be a force of nature or a curse. La Mala Hora translates to 'The Bad Hour,' but what it is depends on who's telling the story, and where they grew up. What also differs regionally is what La Mala Hora is called. The entity goes by a few names, including La Malora, La Malorga, the Evil-Doer, and the Evil One. Witnesses also see the entity as appearing in one of three ways. Some see it appear as a beautiful woman with long, dark hair in either a white or black dress. Usually, the spirit of the woman glides along the side of the road, her feet never touching the ground. Some people claim her face looks like a demon. La Mala Hora's other form is a dark shadow that swirls and spins, changing its shape. The black mass is said to be able to surround a person and disorient them."

"That sounds terrifying," Tate said, resting his elbows on the table, his fingers scratching the scruff on his jaw. Hazel said nothing. She wasn't ready to tell the historian about her run in with the entity.

Paul continued. "According to legend, La Mala Hora could be a demon or an evil spirit. It's so feared throughout New Mexico and Mexico that it rivals fears of the Devil himself. Most of the alleged sightings have taken place along rural roads, usually by travelers who are alone, and almost always near crossroads. As far as what people think it means, seeing La Mala Hora is considered a bad omen, a harbinger of death, but some believe it's a vengeful demon. Most claim those who see La Mala Hora will either be driven insane by the entity or suffocated by its mist."

"Is there any proof to these claims?" Hazel stared at the picture on the table as Tate asked the questions she was too afraid to ask. She was grateful for him being there.

"People have actually been found dead in these areas, but it's hard to know exactly what happened to them, since they were alone in their vehicles. The lucky travelers who escaped their encounters with the lady in white claimed that the fear paralyzed them and that the entity used compulsion over them, hypnotizing them until they had no control over their bodies. There are a few stories of encounters with La Mala Hora, including the one that just made the news. One of the women, distraught over her impending divorce, was visited by police the next morning with news of her husband's murder while he was on a business trip. It was her friends who saw the entity, appearing as a woman with long black hair in a white dress, while on their way to her home so they could keep her company. There are others, like the woman on the news, who had a more volatile interaction with the entity, where it appeared with the face of a demon and attacked their vehicles."

Tate let out a low whistle, leaning back in his chair and running his hand through his hair. "So, what you're telling us is to stay far away from these darkened crossroads?"

Looking back at Paul Sims' face, Hazel waited for his response. She still didn't know if he believed in the stories, or if she did. Even if she'd seen the entity herself, she still didn't know if it was truly a harbinger of death or just another spirit.

"I think the worst thing you'll find on darkened roads at night are wild animals standing on the highway, threatening to run you off the road. As far as La Mala Hora, I can't say whether it's real. I'm not sure if anyone can."

Chapter Twenty-One

The Ghost Patrol

When they left the library, Hazel left with a hollow feeling in her chest. She didn't know if it was fear or something else, but the stories of the infamous urban legend did nothing to steady her heartbeat. Just as she buckled her seatbelt, Tate turned to look at her before starting the car.

"So, that was a lot."

Nodding, she picked at her fingernails. "Yeah. The stories of this thing make it sound so much worse than I'd realized. Let's just hope most of the stories aren't real."

Tate smirked, starting the engine and taking the car out of park. "People are known to exaggerate this sort of thing."

She knew it was the truth, but the photos and testimonials still made her anxiety worse. "I need a drink."

Before taking her first step into the world of ghost hunting, a step she never intended to take, they made their way to a Mexican restaurant known for its happy hour specials. With Tate driving, she could have one—or four—margaritas without endangering anything but her pride. As long as she could speak clearly to the paranormal group, without alcohol-laced mumbling, she'd be okay.

Candy and Jake had already returned to Hazel's side by the time they'd pulled out of the library parking lot, manifesting their forms into the backseat of the car. It was almost as though Candy could feel it in her nonexistent bones that her best friend intended to drink and didn't want to miss the opportunity to be a bad influence.

The group of four left the restaurant just as the sun was starting to set over the arid landscape. Hazel had limited herself to one large margarita, minus the occasional sips taken by Tate. Although drinking a few would have made her mind lighter, she didn't want it to be so light that it left her head altogether, along with her dinner. She wasn't exactly a heavyweight drinker, nor was she a graceful one.

They'd set a neutral location to meet the ghost hunting group, somewhere closer to the crossroads where La Mala Hora was said to be. The hollowness in Hazel's chest seemed to take on a life of its own as they traveled, a familiar feeling of dread that she didn't know how to soothe. She realized all of it could have been in her head, having a tendency toward anxiety as it was, but this felt different.

When they arrived back at the crossroads, a big black van with the words "Ghost Patrol" in white letters was already parked on the shoulder. There were cameras and equipment set up, scattered from the side of the road, all the way into the tree line. Hazel clenched her jaw as she climbed out of the car, hoping no one would get run over by a vehicle that night. It certainly would have been fitting if someone did.

One of the men, short and stocky with a full beard and mustache, set down a large black case and walked toward them. Wearing a flannel shirt and ripped jeans, he wouldn't have been out of place in the grunge movement of the nineties. Jake and Candy moved alongside them, probably plotting how to make the ghost crew's equipment go hay-wire at the most inopportune moment. Hazel had already given them a preemptive scolding, but Candy never paid much mind to that sort of thing. The redheaded spirit usually did whatever she wanted to do; consequences be damned.

"Hazel?" The man eyed Tate warily as he reached for Hazel's hand. She didn't blame him. Tate was at least a foot taller than he was. Thankfully, her husband's smile always disarmed anyone he met.

Taking the man's hand, Hazel gave him a half-hearted handshake. Formalities were never really her thing. "That's me."

"Great! My name is Ryan Hawthorne. I'm the leader of Ghost Patrol." Smiling, he pointed to-ward the woman who was running wires from a camera to a black box sitting on the ground near the van. "That's my wife, Jamie. She's the only woman in our group, and she regrets it every day. The guy over there with the Slayer t-shirt is Jack. He doesn't talk much, but we're pretty sure he can." Ryan chuckled and drew their attention to the area nearest the trees. "I'm just playing around. The old man who looks like he's a member of ZZ Top is Mitch, but he goes by Merlin. Don't ask. It's a long story."

Hazel was giggling internally at Ryan's description of his crew, but Tate's snort was unmistakable, and Candy laughed so hard it was distracting. Thankfully, Ryan and his crew seemed none the wiser. They may have liked to look for ghosts with their equipment, but they didn't have the sixth sense like she did. She didn't have any proof, but Hazel was ninety-nine percent sure that Ryan had a Dungeons and Dragons set in his basement.

Leading them to the van, what Ryan called the "battle station," they had to navigate around wires running across the ground as though they were looking for landmines. She didn't know what most of the equipment was, but it looked expensive. Hopefully, some of that equipment would be able to back up her own experiences, possibly capturing evidence of what was out there.

"Jamie is setting up trap cameras in the trees, as well as one that points toward the highway and another pointing down the shoulder in all directions. If anything manifests into a physical form in front of one, the camera will shoot a picture." Looking up from her task, Ryan's wife smiled at them. Hazel returned the gesture.

Continuing to move through the jumble of equipment, Ryan showed them night vision cameras, EMF meters (which apparently could pick up electromagnetic fields that he claimed ghosts emit), and a collection of tape recorders. There were other items he showed to them, but Hazel was having a hard time taking it all in. She wasn't exactly tech savvy, and she had always refrained from watching ghost hunters on television, for obvious reasons.

The equipment she was most nervous about was something called a spirit box. According to Ryan, the strange box would scan through radio stations in quick succession, and spirits would be able to speak through the sounds. If there was any piece of equipment that was screaming for Candy to toy with it, it was the spirit box. It made Hazel think back to when she'd been abducted by Raymond Waters, and Candy had found a way to speak through Tate's police scanner. The unwanted memory hovered in Hazel's mind for just a moment before she pushed it away.

Having already explained some of her abilities, as well as her La Mala Hora encounters with Ryan on the phone that morning, she knew he would want to test out her claims. Even with that expectation, she had no intention of revealing everything to him. She didn't want him to know about her premonitions of the plane crash, or the unexplainable way in which she'd received them. It wasn't something she wanted to scream from the rooftops, at least not yet. A living child infesting her mind to give her clues about impending tragedies was not a story most would believe, so she tucked that detail away. Plus, she needed to protect Bella.

With that being said, Hazel realized she may have been unable to stop the crash. It was probably the most likely scenario, but she wasn't ready to throw in the towel and return to Louisiana just yet.

"We're going to set out reflector cones on this lane of the highway to let oncoming traffic know we're working here, but this stretch of roadway does tend to be pretty quiet at night. If there was ever a place where La Mala Hora would haunt, this would probably be it."

Hazel nodded as she scanned the stretch of highway, memories of their crash, and her visions in the blackness of her mind, coming back to remind her of the dangers. "When do we get started?"

"Just as soon as it's lights out. We've got about another thirty minutes before sunset, so I'm going to finish setting up, but you and your husband are welcome to sit behind the monitors and familiarize yourself with the equipment. As long as you don't break anything."

Ryan smiled, but she wasn't so sure she should be trusted with any of it. "I can't make any promises."

CHAPTER TWENTY-TWO

The Lady in White

Hazel tried to familiarize herself with some of the equipment. She really did. But after one of the black devices with flashing lights seemed to go crazy on her, she dropped it like a hot potato and pretended she'd never even touched it. It had only taken a few moments before Candy and Jake burst into laughter next to her, all but telling her they'd done it.

Scowling, she flipped them off. She was civilized, after all. "You two are like middle schoolers. I really do want to see if we can get real evidence of La Mala Hora tonight, or the spirits I keep seeing, evidence aside from my own experiences, so I would *appreciate it* if you two would run off and play. Go have sex in the woods or something. Geez."

Tate chuckled, but Candy seemed to think it was a good idea and grabbed her boyfriend's hand, dragging him into the forest. "Let me guess...they ran off?"

Shaking her head, she smirked at her husband. "Even though you can't see them, you still know her so well."

The group of ghost hunters finished their setup as the sky darkened, and moved on to fidget with their equipment, settling into their stations for the night. Hazel was clueless, but they at least appeared to know what they were doing.

Tension hung in the air, but she didn't know if it was because of her own fears or because of what was lurking in the darkness. Just as she was starting to look for the entity she was there to find, Ryan approached them from the tree line.

"Ready?" he asked, grabbing one of the little black devices with all the lights and that intimidating spirit box from the table.

Hazel cleared her throat, her chest already tightening. "I guess I'm as ready as I'm going to be. What do we do first?"

Ryan gave Tate one more unsure glance before pointing toward the shoulder of the crossroads. "Since it's quiet out right now, you and I can go down there and have a spirit box and EVP session... just to see if anything comes up."

Having little idea what any of that entailed, Hazel smiled anyway and followed him as he led her toward the place where she and Tate had wrecked their rental car only days before. Tate remained sitting at the table, but Hazel could tell he was hesitant about letting her walk away. Just him being there made her feel safer, even if he wasn't within arm's reach. She scanned the area for Candy, as well as any other spirits, but she saw nothing as they neared the crossroads. Part of her was glad, but she knew that was the part she shouldn't listen to. That part of her wouldn't solve the mystery and prevent a tragic plane crash.

There were two folding chairs set up on the shoulder near the intersection, so they were able to sit down facing the crossroads. Ryan set the spirit box on the ground before turning to face her.

Handing Hazel a tape recorder, the excitement in the ghost hunter's eyes was clear. He expected her to bring ghosts to him that night, but she cringed to think what else she may attract. "So, you're just going to hold this and talk as you normally would. Then we'll go back and listen to it so we can see if anything came through. Sometimes the spirits won't talk if there are multiple people around. I'll leave if I have to, but we can try it like this for now."

Hazel nodded, examining the tape recorder as though it were a foreign object. She'd used tape recorders many times in her career as a public defender, but never to speak to spirits. She'd never had to. Scanning the night covered roadway again, she still saw nothing. Even the insects were quiet. Ryan pulled out the EVP reader from his pocket, setting it down on the ground by her feet. There was only a brief moment, just as she was about to turn the tape recorder on, before a swirling dark mass enveloped her and everything went black.

The plane moved through the air at a leisurely pace, the passengers comfortable in their seats as they passed the time. Hazel sat in the second to last row, right next to Bella. The little girl had her hair in pigtails again, with huge red bows around each, nearly swallowing her head.

"You found me again, Hazel. My daddy just finished reading a bedtime story to me. Do you want to know what story? I can tell you about it."

Head still in a daze, Hazel scanned the plane. What was she doing right before she arrived here? She couldn't remember. "What plane is this, Bella? Do you know the company?"

Head tilting, the little girl seemed surprised. It took her a moment to reply. "Oh, I'm not sure. You know, I've never been on a real plane before?"

Hazel didn't have the capacity to listen to Bella, not on this night. She had little doubt the child could talk for days if she let her.

The first wave of turbulence hit, tossing a few pieces of luggage from the overhead bins. "Bella. This is important. I need to stop this plane from crashing."

Grimacing, the child looked around the plane again as though she'd forgotten where they were, or maybe she was looking for someone. "I'm sorry, Hazel. You can't stop it."

Heart dropping into her stomach, Hazel leaned forward in her seat, bracing as another jolt hit the aircraft. "What do you mean I can't stop the crash? Isn't that why you've been bringing me here?" Urgency filled Hazel's chest, the familiar fight-or-flight response making her heart race as she looked for an exit.

Bella only shrugged, turning to look behind the seat as she fumbled with the hem of her red and white dress.

"Bella, what are you looking for?" Hazel looked over the backs of their seats as well, frantically needing to solve the puzzle, but she saw nothing. No one. She didn't understand.

"I was looking for the lady." Bella's tone was so nonchalant that it threatened to flare Hazel's nonexistent temper. It was like the little girl didn't care that the plane was going to crash and kill everyone on board. Running her hands down her face, Hazel tried to calm her expression. She had to remember that she was dealing with a small child, even if Bella's knowing abilities made her seem so much older.

"Bella. What lady are you looking for?"

As though on cue, the lights of the plane went out, all the passengers merely memories in the darkness.

Bella pointed toward the front of the plane, where a familiar black cloud churned toward them, the hint of a white dress peeking out through the swirls. "The lady who said you can't stop the crash. She said the spirits are already hers. They all are."

Chapter Twenty-Three
The Breaking Point

"Hazel. Wake up, sweetie. Come on. Wake up." Grogginess plagued Hazel as her eyes fluttered open to see Tate hovering over her, his hand on her shoulder as he cradled her in his lap. The ground was uncomfortable against her back, the stones digging into her skin. "There you are. Does anything hurt?" She tried to sit up, but a gentle hand held her in place. It was a familiar situation. "Not yet, sweetie. Just lay here for a minute."

Clearing her throat, she looked around, but it was too dark to see much more than Candy hovering nearby. Her best friend was curled into Jake as she watched Hazel, her big blue eyes even wider than usual. The chair she'd been sitting in was toppled to the ground beside her. "What happened?"

Tate ran his fingers through his hair. His face was etched with worry, making her feel guilty. She kept ending up in this similar situation, no matter how much she wanted to avoid it. "You passed out again."

Only a moment passed before Tate lifted her up, an arm supporting her back and the other beneath her knees and began to carry her toward the car. "Wait. We can't leave yet. Tate. The plane's going to crash."

She had never seen Tate's face so contorted before. Worry mixed with absolute frustration. It sent a sinking feeling into her chest that she'd never felt before. *Was he angry with her?*

Ignoring her plea, he set her down in the passenger's seat and slammed the car door closed before walking to the driver's side and climbing in. Normally, she would've probably gotten out of the car and went back to where her answers were, but she didn't dare, not with the look on his face. Tate was worth more than anything. Even Candy and

Jake stayed away, realizing it was a private moment between them.

When he got back into the car, he gripped the wheel, his hands white knuckled as he loosened a breath. "You know I support you." His voice was so calm that it unsettled her. There was a but... She knew it was coming. "But this has got to stop." When he turned to face her, his eyes were glassy. Her heart shattered into a million pieces. "I'm not asking you to never help spirits again, but this case is too much. You passing out all over the place? On the side of the road? The crash?" Heart hovering somewhere outside of her chest, she just stared. There was nothing she could say. "Sweetie... this is not okay. I'm fucking worried about you. I love you too much to let you put yourself in danger."

Tears broke from her eyes at the sight of Tate crying. It was something she'd never seen before, a sight she never wanted to see again. "I'm so sorry I put you through this." When she reached for his hand, taking it from the steering wheel, he let her. Pulling her into him, he wrapped his arms around her so tight it felt like she'd never get free, but she didn't want to.

"Don't be sorry. Just say you won't keep allowing them to pull you in like this." All she could do was nod and sob. It was such a helpless feeling to be so torn between two worlds, between her love for her husband and her obligation since birth to help the spirits. But the living had to come before the dead. It was a mantra she'd have to remind herself when it became too much. "I'm going to get you out of here. Out of this city. I'm taking you home."

Letting him go to wipe her face with a napkin, Hazel gave only a slight glance out of the window. "I'd like that. Before we leave, though, can you please do something for me?"

"Anything, except for letting you go back out there."

"Please urge Ryan and the crew to leave right now. That plane's going to crash, and I'm afraid it's going to land here."

Tate didn't hesitate, jumping out of the car and running toward the black van where everyone was standing by to make sure she was okay. She couldn't hear what they were saying, but she was relieved when they sprang into action, gathering up their supplies quickly and piling them into the van. When Tate returned to their car and pulled onto the highway, the Ghost Patrol van was behind them.

Tate clung to her hand as they made their way back to their hotel, as though she would disappear if he let her go. Candy and Jake had not returned, but that wasn't surprising. Even if Candy usually had bad timing when she popped in on them, often purposely, she was considerate enough to stay away in such a situation. Candy and Jake had been murdered by the same woman; a woman who had been obsessed with Jake. After all they'd gone through, her best friend was well familiar with what it meant for a couple to need space so they could work through shit. They were probably following close by or had moved back to the hotel. Either way, Hazel didn't expect to see them again that night.

Although there was relief in Hazel's body since leaving the crossroads and getting cleaned up, she couldn't help the tightness in her chest as they watched the local news, expecting to see news of a plane crash, but hoping they wouldn't. Everything in her told her she was right. It was going to happen, and she couldn't prevent it.

They watched the muted television for what seemed like hours as she cuddled into Tate's chest, his muscular arms wrapped around her as he ran fingers through her hair. They talked about the next day, how they would make the trip to her parents' ranch to say goodbye, and then would start driving back to Louisiana. The sooner they could get back to their life, the better. They'd left the state to get married and enjoy their honeymoon, but the trip had turned out way different from what they'd planned.

"Are you mad at me?" She didn't want the answer, but she still needed to ask. The pain of what had transpired in the car stayed with her, a bruise in her chest that would take a while to heal. Even with all her self-doubt about whether she was good enough for him, she'd never seen him genuinely angry with her. He may have only been mad at the situation, but it still cut all the same.

Tate scanned her face as his fingers traced down her jaw. "I'm not mad at you, sweetie. I've never been mad at you. I just don't like you ending up in these situations. It's not safe. I can handle a lot, but I can't handle you getting hurt."

She tried to absorb his words, tried to let them infiltrate the darkest places of her consciousness, but the wound still throbbed. Reading it on her face, he kissed her. The warmth of his skin, the taste of him, loosened the knot, untangling all the strings that had wound themselves together inside her chest. She dug her fingers into the muscles of his shoulders, assuring herself of how solid he was. The spirits couldn't cost her Tate. He *was* her whole life. Their kiss deepened, his body sliding over hers, filling her with the familiar electricity he'd always elicited. She was so taken in the moment, drifting into the world where she wanted to be, that she'd almost missed the incessant vibration of her cellphone on the side table. A string yanked inside of her, the knot tightening enough to take her breath away.

Pulling away from Tate only a little, careful not to make him climb off her, she reached for her phone. "I'm sorry, baby. Let me just check in case it's an emergency from my mom."

Tate nodded, leaning on his elbow as he waited patiently for her to return her attention to him. She would give him all he wanted after she checked to make sure it wasn't urgent.

Unlocking the screen of her phone, Hazel's hand lost grip on the device, dropping it to the floor. The pounding of her heart was too loud within her ears, sounding like the roar of an engine. She was still for a moment, leaning on her side as she stared into space, bile rising in her throat and threatening to make her vomit.

Tate jumped from the bed, grabbing her phone and unlocking it quickly. She heard his gasp, but it didn't register. When he climbed back onto the bed, wrapping his arms around her, her mind still felt like it was out of her body. She gagged, holding her stomach down, but just barely. Tate held up the phone again, scanning the message where she could see it. It was from her mom, but it wasn't about her father.

All the message said was, "*A passenger plane went down near Holy Ghost Campground an hour ago.*"

CHAPTER TWENTY-FOUR
The Crash

Time stood still as Hazel stared at the screen of her phone, at the ominous message her mother had sent her. She didn't even know why her mother was awake at such an hour, but Sandi had similar abilities to her, so it was possible her mother had been woken by something innate, some supernatural force telling her that souls needed help.

Tate took charge when Hazel couldn't, responding to her mother before grabbing his own phone to message the detective. They hadn't heard back from Detective Bourgeois since his last message, but neither of them was surprised. Everything had happened too fast for anyone to prevent the crash.

She knew that in her mind, even if some part of her hated herself for not stopping it from happening.

Leaving their phones on the bed near them, Tate pulled her against his chest, tipping her eyes up to meet his. "This isn't your fault. Do you hear me? You couldn't have prevented this."

She heard him, but the words didn't quite register. Whether or not she could have prevented the crash, there was nothing she could do now that the incident had already happened. Well, nothing aside from helping any spirits who hadn't crossed through to where they belonged, or to wherever the black mass would take them. The thought of the mysterious entity luring the dead anywhere unsettled her, but what could she do about it? With the investigation and cleanup at the crash site, she wouldn't be able to go to the scene for weeks. Possibly longer. She truly was helpless.

Blinking rapidly, Hazel tried to pull herself into the present, the present with Tate, and not the present that was happening miles away. "I'm trying to accept that. It just may take a while."

Tate nodded and kissed her forehead, the warmth of his lips lingering. "Just know how much I love you, and I understand." Her body warmed as he leaned in to kiss her lips. "Just know that there's nothing we can do about any of this. My plans haven't changed. I'm still taking you home."

Allowing him to pull her into his chest, she closed her eyes, the exhaustion of the past days draining her energy and leaving behind the shell of someone too tired to fight. Sleep took her before she had a chance to think about anything else.

The next morning was flooded with news of the crash, although the authorities were still trying to figure out what had caused it. Sixty-seven souls were on that plane, and not one survived.

The grief was a physical entity, sitting like a black cloud next to Hazel all morning. Tate looked after her, fussing over her like he had after she'd been rescued from Raymond Waters' cabin of horrors in the Louisiana swamp. She let him. She didn't have any energy to take care of herself, anyway.

They left the hotel as soon as they woke, grabbing breakfast and coffee from a drive thru, before heading toward her parents' ranch. The food tasted like sawdust in her mouth, but she forced herself to chew and swallow, a robotic function meant to keep her from vomiting all over the car. She didn't know how much she had to lose, but she figured her stomach could dig something up if given the chance.

Candy and Tate returned to them that morning, both horrified at the developments. As Hazel suspected, the pair had returned to the hotel once she and Tate drove away from the crossroads. Candy admitted to peeking into their hotel room hours later, but they'd both been asleep by that point, so she didn't bother them.

The offer stood open for them to stay the night at her parents' home, but Hazel had no interest in doing so. Tate admitted the same. Any minute they stayed in Santa Fe that day was a minute too long. So, after a brief lunch with her parents, they left for their sixteen-hour drive back to Louisiana. Sure, they'd have to stop overnight, and the rental car would cost a fortune when they left it in a new location, but it didn't matter. Although Hazel realized flying truly was a safe way to travel, she couldn't bring herself to do it. At least not yet.

Stopping in a rural Texas town that Hazel couldn't name, they trudged into their hotel room and fell asleep as soon as they hit the pillow. They'd both showered, but she was so exhausted that the entire ordeal had been a blur. Her mother updated her on news about the crash, but there had still been no update on the cause. With the ongoing investigation, it was unlikely the authorities would make those details public after only one day. The cause didn't matter, anyway. At least not to Hazel. No matter why the plane had crashed, she'd failed those people, even if she was powerless to stop it.

Waking up the following morning, she was surprised to have not been haunted by any nightmares, or any visits from Bella. It was possible that the crash had ended those particular communications, but she didn't want to place any bets on it. Her interactions with the spirit world had rarely ever gone as planned. She was glad to have gotten a semi-restful night of sleep, no matter what the reasoning for their silence was.

When she and Tate left the hotel room for the last leg of their journey to New Orleans, they were both beyond tired of being away from home. Candy and Jake had popped up in the backseat halfway to Austin, bringing a bit of entertainment as Candy sang along, albeit loudly, to the radio. Candy truly was an entertaining woman, even after death.

Things rarely seemed to bother her. Or if they did, she didn't let it show.

Knowing that Hazel was in a difficult place, no one tried to fool her into thinking otherwise. They were simply supportive, which she appreciated. Tate and Candy were exactly who she needed in her life. Jake was always a neutral party, which she appreciated all the same.

A collective breath left them when they crossed the Luling Bridge, which brought them close to their neighborhood. Candy and Jake had faded out somewhere around Baton Rouge, tired of the drive and having no reason to withstand it. Unfortunately for Hazel and Tate, they had no choice but to keep trucking along.

It was a surreal experience for her to return to their home as a married woman, a home that hadn't been hers for very long but seemed like it had been forever. Her relationship with Tate had been a whirlwind romance, a friendship that blossomed over seven years to become something that would last forever. Even with the spirit obligations she knew would find her later, there was no place she would have rather been than in their home. When she laid in bed that night, she did so wrapped in the arms of a man who would withstand any storm with her and would put his foot down when the winds became too dangerous.

Epilogue

It's Not Over

*T*he sound of the television came into focus, and the smell of her mother's vanilla
candle made its way to her nose before Hazel
could see the visual of where she was. She
walked through her parents' ranch, not knowing where she was going, but simply following
the signs of life. She wasn't sure why she was
seeing the home. She and Tate had been back
in New Orleans for a week, settling into their
lives as a married couple, which hadn't changed
their lives much at all.

There was a familiar pundit on the television,
making claims about things he had no knowledge of, just to influence the public. She and
Tate didn't watch the program, but she was still

familiar with it. Stepping forward, as though she was moving with a purpose, Hazel entered the den.

Darkened by night, the only light in the room came from the television. Her mother was nowhere in sight, but her father was sitting on the sofa, remote in his hand, and a sleepy look on his face.

Having been through the situation before, she didn't even attempt to speak to him, because she knew he wouldn't be able to hear her. She wasn't really there. Instead, Hazel sat on the chair opposite her father and watched him. Aside from the hospital bed, and the brief visit after he'd been discharged, she hadn't been in the same room with her father for five years. Even if he couldn't see her, she still wanted to take the chance to be with him. She didn't know when she would be able to do so again.

They sat there for a while; her watching him and him watching the television. She wasn't sure how much time had passed before her father yawned, stretched his back, and took a step toward the hallway.

A tiny voice entered her head as she watched his movements, a familiar voice that made her skin crawl. She couldn't see Bella, but she heard her warning. "It's not over."

Only a moment passed before her father, still making his way through the doorway, collapsed onto the floor.

Shooting up from her seat, Hazel darted toward him, dropping to the floor beside her father.

"Mom! Hurry! Something's wrong!" She screamed to her mother as she cried, her voice meeting no ears but her own. Holding onto his chest, Roman grunted in pain, trying to lift himself, only to fall back onto the carpet.

Desperate, hoping her mother's abilities were honed enough to see her, Hazel headed in the direction of the kitchen. She'd only taken a few steps before the figure in the hallway blocked her path, the darkness enveloping her until the vision faded into oblivion.

To be continued...

Enjoyed Crossroads of Darkness?

The afterword is an opportunity for the author to offer any final explanations about the book, and is most common in non-fiction. Some books include this as part of the body content whereas others will place it in the back matter.

Follow C.A. Varian

Sign up for C. A. Varian's newsletter to receive current updates on her new and upcoming releases, sales, and giveaways:

You can also find all stories, books, and social media pages and follow her here:

https://linktr.ee/cavarian

https://cavarian.com

Also By

Hazel Watson Mystery Series
Kindred Spirits: Prequel
The Sapphire Necklace
Justice for the Slain
Whispers from the Swamp
Crossroads of Death
The Spirit Collector (coming October 2023)

Crown of the Phoenix Series
Crown of the Phoenix
Crown of the Exiled
Crown of the Prophecy (Coming Soon)
Mate of the Phoenix

Supernatural Savior Series
Song of Death

Goddess of Death

An Other World Series
The Other World
The Other Key
The Other Fate (coming January 2024)

My Alien Mate Series
My Alien Protector

Saving Scarlett (coming January 2024)

Second Chance with Santa (coming December 2024)

About the Author

Raised in a small town in the heart of Louisiana's Cajun Country, C. A. Varian spent most of her childhood fishing, crabbing, and getting sunburnt at the beach. Her love of reading began very young, and she would often compete at school to read enough books to earn prizes.

Graduating with the first of her college degrees as a mother of two in her late twenties, she became a public-school teacher. As of the release of this book, she was finally able to resign from teaching to write full time!

Writing became a passion project, and she put out her first novel in 2021, and has continued to publish new novels every few months since then, not slowing down for even a minute.

Married to a retired military officer, she spent many years moving around for his career, but they now live in central Alabama, with her youngest daughter, Arianna. Her oldest daughter, Brianna, is enjoying her happily ever after with her new husband and several pups. C. A. Varian has two Shih Tzus that she considers her children. Boy, Charlie, and girl, Luna, are their mommy's shadows. She also has three cats named Ramses, Simba, and Cookie.